"So what are you going to do, Dee?"

Mike eyed her impassively. "Are you going to keep running, or are you going to come with me?"

"And if I decide to keep running?"

"Then I follow." There was no hesitation.

"Why don't you go away?"

"Why don't you go home? There are a lot of people worried about you."

"Don't give me that nonsense!" Dee burst out angrily. "They're only worried about my money—that's all they want from me!" She looked around the crowded truck stop at the reassuring drivers who'd offered her their rough-and-ready friendship. "I'm never going back there, and if you try to force me—well, don't say I didn't warn you, Mr. Carridine!"

Books by Amanda Carpenter

HARLEQUIN PRESENTS
703—THE WALL
735—THE GREAT ESCAPE

HARLEQUIN ROMANCES
2605—A DEEPER DIMENSION
2648—A DAMAGED TRUST

These books may be available at your local bookseller.

For a list of all titles currently available,
send your name and address to:

Harlequin Reader Service
P.O. Box 52040, Phoenix, AZ 85072-2040
Canadian address: P.O. Box 2800, Postal Station A,
5170 Yonge St., Willowdale, Ont. M2N 5T5

AMANDA CARPENTER

the great escape

Harlequin Books

TORONTO • NEW YORK • LONDON
AMSTERDAM • PARIS • SYDNEY • HAMBURG
STOCKHOLM • ATHENS • TOKYO • MILAN

Harlequin Presents first edition November 1984
ISBN 0-373-10735-8

Original hardcover edition published in 1984
by Mills & Boon Limited

Printed in U.S.A.

CHAPTER ONE

DEE careered around the corner of the wall that effectively shielded the restaurant's customer's view of the back, and she skidded for a moment on wet, newly washed floor. Then, as her rubber-soled shoes gripped the tile, she catapulted past the employees' break area and burst into the women's dressing room, silver-blonde hair flying around her head in a golden tangled aureole. After a first, surprised stare, Kim, the head waitress, who had been sitting and smoking at the break table, rose hastily and hurried to the door that Dee had disappeared into, knocking on it worriedly.

'Hey, babe, are you okay?' she called out. She was a large, rather heavy girl, with long brown hair that was presently twisted into a knot at the nape of her neck. The knot was beginning to slide to one side, giving her an untidy appearance.

'No!' Dee shouted, the sound muffled through the closed door.

Kim tried the door and found it locked. She knocked again, harder. 'C'mon now, Dee! Open up and let me in. Is Kathy watching the floor while you're back here?'

'Yes!' she shouted again, and there was an instant of silence before the door opened swiftly. Dee peered out at Kim with huge, dilated blue eyes. 'Get in here!' she hissed, and Kim found herself unexpectedly dragged into the room as Dee reached out one small hand and yanked her in by the shoulder strap. The door slammed shut behind them both. After hauling the other girl in so precipitously, Dee backed away and surveyed her warily. She had her locker wide open, and her street clothes were spilled out of it. A canvas knapsack lay on

5

the floor. She whirled, pulled on a pair of faded blue
jeans over her slim legs and zipped them up. Then she
reached behind her and unbuttoned her uniformed
skirt, throwing it carelessly into a corner and tugging on
a plain cotton blouse. Off came the white work shoes
and she started to pull on diminutive tennis shoes. By
that time Kim had begun to come out of her shock.

'God, Dee!' she gasped incredulously, ogling the
smaller, slight girl. 'What the hell are you doing? Do
you want to get fired?'

'I'm going home sick!' Dee snapped, tugging
frantically at her shoelace that had become knotted. All
her movements were suggesting a feeling of urgency and
haste, and this finally began to register with the older
girl, who began to look even more worried than before.

'Listen, kiddo, if you're in some kind of trouble, I
think you'd better tell me about it,' Kim said slowly,
narrowing her eyes and lowering her brows.

Dee was perched on a shipping crate that doubled as
the only seat in the tiny changing room and she had her
head bent over the knot as her thin fingers worked
furiously to get it loose. The strings came untied, she
slipped the shoe on, and then she looked up, blonde
hair falling into her eyes and making her look like a
tousled English sheepdog puppy. The blue eyes peered
out of the hair until she shoved it back impatiently.
'Kim, you've got to try and cover for me with Brett.
Tell him I suddenly got violently sick and I had to go
home,' she pleaded hurriedly. 'Tell him I died—I don't
care what you tell him, but just let me go home!'

The older girl leaned thoughtfully against the wall,
her eyes never leaving Dee's face. 'Just what happened?'
she asked quietly.

'I—I can't tell you all of it,' Dee stammered out
nervously, her hands plucking at her small knapsack.
'I'm in trouble. I haven't done anything wrong or
illegal, but I am in trouble, and this fellow has been

looking for me for a long time. He just walked into the restaurant, and—he can't find me! I just happened to look outside and I saw him, so I was able to tell Kathy to tell him that I'd gone home sick before he came inside ... Kim, I have to leave, whether it's all right or not—I have to! Call Sherry—she'd come in to work the rest of my shift. I'll bet Brett can't get too angry if she's in working when he gets back.'

'I don't know about that,' Kim replied, chewing her lower lip. 'When he gets back and finds you gone, he's going to hit the roof. It won't matter if you were really sick or not, he'll just be mad that you went without waiting to ask him first.'

Dee started to shove the rest of her things either into her knapsack or into her locker, jamming the combination lock on afterwards. She hadn't really expected to be feeling this hunted dread again, and that old familiar nervous churning in her stomach was back. Her jaw angled out stubbornly. 'I don't care if he gets mad or not,' she uttered grimly. 'I've got to go. I don't have much time!'

Kim watched her, puzzled and wry. 'All I have to say is that it's a good thing you're a favourite of Sammy's,' she said, dryness tingeing her voice as she mentioned the restaurant's manager. Brett was only the assistant manager and couldn't fire anyone without Sammy's approval. 'You just might get away with this madness and still have a job left.'

'Oh, shoot!' Dee skidded to a stop outside the dressing room at Kim's words. 'I'd better write Sammy a note of explanation, just in case. Can I borrow your pen? I locked mine up with my uniform.' She took the pen that Kim proffered her and scribbled madly on a paper napkin, biting the end of the pen from time to time and grimacing.

'Just in case of what?' the other girl asked her curiously. Although she would never admit it to anyone, she was very envious of the younger girl. Dee was something of a mystery to most of the restaurant staff at Dandy's, and though no one but Sammy knew very much about her, she was well liked by everyone for her cheerful, pert manner, and hard work.

Dee hesitated fractionally before answering. She had thoughtlessly said what had been on her mind, meaning just in case she wasn't able to come back, but she couldn't tell Kim that. 'Why, just in case he really gets angry, of course.' Sammy was the only one she had told the whole truth to, because she had wanted him to know and understand in case something like this were to happen. He was a gentle, kind man in his forties, and he had an abundance of patience. Dee had instinctively trusted him ever since he had hired her. His sympathy and understanding had meant a great deal to her in the past. When she finished the note, she taped it shut to avoid curious perusal from anyone but him, then handed it over to Kim as an added safety measure. 'Could you see that nobody but Sammy gets this?'

Kim knew what she had meant and grinned. Aside from Sammy, Kim was the person who knew the most about her, which wasn't much. Dee found her trustworthy and loyal, and if she was at times a bit too crude for Dee's taste—well, that was the restaurant business, and it was overlooked for friendship's sake. 'You mean, see that Sammy gets it and not Brett, is that it?' she replied with a short laugh. 'My pleasure, sugar. Now, let me go out to the front and see if that fellow is still here before you take off.' She turned to go and bumped right into Kathy, who had come up behind the two of them. 'What're you doing back here? Now who's watching the floor?'

Kathy, a tall, gangly girl with a wide, wide smile, answered, 'Jerry is watching the door while he mops. That guy is gone, Dee. He left a few minutes ago, but I couldn't come back to tell you because I had an order to take out. He probably will be back in as soon as he finds that you aren't at home like I told him you'd be. I lied and said you didn't have a telephone.' She looked from one girl to the other, curiously. 'She's leaving without asking Brett? I don't want to be around when the explosion comes.'

'It can't be helped,' Kim sighed, still watching Dee. She smiled. 'You'd better skip along, darlin'. I'd say you have about twenty minutes before he's back here asking us embarrassing questions. If he talks to Brett, we're all goners.'

Dee wanted to let go of her control and sink into the panic that threatened her calm, but she couldn't let herself. She'd come too far to make any stupid mistakes now, and the most important thing was to keep her wits about her. 'Thanks, you two,' she said, and impulsively threw her arms around them each, hugging hard. Surprised, embarrassed, and quite touched, the two girls hugged her back briefly before pushing her away.

'Hey, cut that out, kiddo! Anyone would think you were going to your death, the way you're acting now!' Kim laughed, although she couldn't help the strange look she sent to Kathy. 'Do you—need any money or anything? I've got something stuck in the bank that I can help you out with. You aren't in debt, are you?'

The irony of that made Dee snort a mirthless laugh. 'No, I've got plenty, thanks. I just have to stay away from that man we saw—Kathy, will you remember what he looks like in case he's in again to look for me?'

That made the other girl chuckle heartily. 'Dee, sometimes you say the silliest things! I'd remember that man any time ... don't tell me you don't find him handsome? He'd be good for it, wouldn't he?'

Kim emitted a groan. 'And I had to miss him! I'll have to be sure to keep an eye out in front, in case he does come along!' The two laughed together, while Dee winced.

'I suppose he's good-looking, if you go for the hard type. I've just gotten used to thinking of him as being on the other side, I guess. This isn't making much sense to you, I know, and we're wasting time. His name is Mike Carridine, in case he happens to introduce himself, and he's a private investigator. Could you tell him I might have appendicitis, or something, and he might want to check the hospitals, since he missed me at home? He couldn't know that I saw him, and so he won't know that you might be lying. It should keep him busy for a little while, don't you think? I'm going to need all the headstart I can contrive . . . 'bye, Kim, and thanks!'

A few minutes later, Dee stuck her head cautiously around the corner of the employees' entrance, looking around with great care. Finding the back parking lot empty, she ran over to Kim's car and scrabbled at the lock with the key. Then she threw open the door and slid behind the ancient vehicle's wheel, turning the ignition quickly. It roared gustily, the muffler having rusted away some time before, and she knew she was going to have a headache from the fumes by the time she got back to her apartment.

It was nice of Kim to let her borrow the car. They had arranged for Kim to take a cab (on Dee's funds) to Dee's apartment, and she could pick up her car keys from the landlady who lived on the ground floor. That way Dee could leave right away, without waiting for a cab herself.

She had plenty of time to think, as she drove through the downtown of Akron to the cheaper, rougher part of town. She would have to run away, again. It was sad in a way, because she had begun to feel settled in this city. She had spent close to nine months working at Dandy's, and it would hurt to leave her friends. She had managed to put away some money after her few living expenses, and she'd begun to hope that she could go to college in the fall, but

of course now that was out. She would need every penny
that she had saved to relocate herself again. It just might
be enough to see her through until her eighteenth
birthday, just under two months away, if she skimped on
meals. The end was in sight, she knew, but she was so tired
of running and so discouraged at the moment, it didn't
seem to matter any more.

She rolled down the car window to let in the cool
keen wind of March whisk through the confines of the
interior. Kim smoked too much, and the inside of the
car smelled like a tobacco factory. A pothole made the
car lurch, and then she was pulling to a stop just in
front of a red light.

Her hands were shaking. Running away . . . she was
always running away. With a burst of fury she cursed
the man, Mike Carridine, with a round fluency that she
had picked up while working at the restaurant. Then
she laughed, remembering how shocked she had been at
some of the things she'd heard at Dandy's. One gets
accustomed to crudity and swearing fairly quickly, in an
atmosphere like that.

Carridine was good at his job, she'd give him that.
Anyone who could sift through the series of red
herrings and false trails that she had left behind her in
only nine months had to be good, very good. She
hadn't expected him to be so fast. He must be a
bloodhound with a very sensitive nose. She would have
to keep on her toes, keep her head and use her quick
mind to get out of this one.

Nine months ago. She drove automatically as she
thought back, an oddly bitter and ugly twist to her pale
lips. It was a lifetime ago, that nine months, a thousand
lifetimes ago. The thought of giving up and going back
was intolerable.

She shifted the car and in spite of her serious
thoughts, had to chuckle at the very human-like groan
it gave as it accelerated slowly.

She was approaching her street, her eyes alert, wary, searching. She slowed, and then, instinct warning her, pulled over into a gas station lot to call the restaurant quickly. Kim's voice answered briskly, and she cut across the other girl's greeting. 'It's me. Has Carridine been in yet, Kim?'

'Yes,' the other girl answered brightly, 'we do have carry-out. How can I help you?'

Dee thought rapidly at this odd reply. 'He's right there at the counter and you can't say anything, right?' That was good. It meant that she could get to her apartment safely.

'That's right, carry-out coffee is by the cup, no refills,' was the reply. This was going to be frustrating, she could tell.

'Is—is he having coffee? Is that what you meant? Hell, what a way to have a conversation!' she muttered, running her hand through her blonde hair and rumpling it even more. A gas station attendant passed by and leered at her suggestively, so she turned her back to him.

'That's right.'

'Just answer yes or no, and I'll try to ask the right questions . . . did you tell him that I might have appendicitis?'

'Yes.'

'How did he take it—Damn! Did he seem to believe it?' She didn't know what she would do if he didn't believe that one.

'I don't know the price of that. The assistant manager isn't back from the bank yet, so I can't ask him. It's a speciality item and not listed. You could call back in a few minutes, if you'd like.'

'Now what in the world does that mean?' Dee retorted, exasperated. She heard a muffled laugh from the other end of the line. 'You don't know if he swallowed the story or not, and you want me to call back later? How will I know if he's gone or not? You could call me at the apartment as soon as he leaves. D'you have my number?'

'Yes, I think so. I'll just call you then, when I know for sure. He should be back in about five minutes or so.'

'I really could scream,' Dee said conversationally. 'Does that mean that he's almost done with his coffee?' This was not going very coherently.

'. . . there, I've got your number,' Kim told her, voice quivering. She gritted her teeth in frustration. 'I'll give you a call as soon as I find out the price. Thank you.'

Dee bolted out of the phone booth as soon as she had hung up the receiver. She had so very little time! She reversed the car with a loud roar and shot off down the road. A quick turn to the right had her pulled on to her street and soon she was parked beside a large old house with peeling white paint, heading for the front door at a run. It wasn't much of a head start at all, and she was beginning to be swamped by that panic. The feeling of being pursued was nerve-racking, to say the least. It could so easily lead to paranoia.

She called out as she let herself into the house and heard slow shuffling footsteps come down the hallway. Mrs Gordon smiled at her cheerily. 'Why, hello, dear. You're home from work early, aren't you?' she piped brightly. 'There was a nice young man here about a half an hour ago asking for you——'

Dee took a deep breath, for patience. 'I know, Mrs Gordon—he came in at work. Look, I'm not feeling well. Could you do me a favour?'

'Certainly, my dear.'

'Do you remember my friend Kim, from work? These are the keys to her car. She's going to be picking it up later. Could you give them to her?'

'Of course,' the elderly lady replied, taking the keys

in one gnarled hand. 'But aren't you going to be home? If you aren't well, you should——'

'I've got a doctor's appointment,' Dee lied, crossing her fingers childishly behind her back. 'Have to go and get ready—thanks, Mrs Gordon!' She didn't give the old lady any time to react, but hurried up the stairs to her tiny apartment. It was really converted from two bedrooms, with a minuscule bath and kitchenette put in. There was a shower stall with no tub, and it was possible to sit on the stool, reach with one hand to turn on the shower and reach with the other hand to turn on the sink taps. One person could turn around in the tiny space; two was a terrible squeeze.

Her kitchen was as tiny, with a refrigerator that reached her waist and the ancient stove and sink exactly one step away. The kitchen and the bathroom had been built into one of the two bedrooms, and the other was her living area, with a single bed doubling as a couch, with huge throw pillows against the wall as the back. She had a portable television on a stand across the room and green potted plants all over the place.

It wasn't quite the Ritz, but it was cheap and well within her budget, and she had decorated it in yellows, browns and oranges with, of course, the green from the plants. One entire wall held her paperback collection, the one luxury that she had allowed herself with the money left over from paying her bills. All the rest of the money had gone into the bank.

Once inside, she didn't waste any time. Her movements were brisk, quick, and economical. She whisked around the small apartment, pulling out her suitcase and all the clothes on hangers. She threw it all on the couch-cum-bed and then went to make a quick call to a taxi company, making arrangements for a cab to come around in half an hour. Then she started throwing things in the open suitcase, practice and adrenalin making her swift.

While her hands were busy, her thoughts were too, vivid images from the past coming before her attention. Would she have run away if she had known how hard it was going to be? Who could really know that for sure? She rather thought she would have, though. As she remembered, she hadn't really had any choice.

All the same, she had been just seventeen when she had left, with no notion of how to handle herself or how to handle life in the working world. All she could remember was that things had just got to be too much to handle, staying. That terrible feeling of being trapped, being lonely, being isolated—it all came back to her too vividly.

The night she particularly remembered with a nightmarish clarity of past pain and despair had been the breaking point.

Dee stared outside at the miserable wet darkness. Inside it was just as dark, for she had the lights off in her large bedroom. Depression gloomed in her young mind like a big black spider. Her heart ached. She was tired, and it always seemed that she was tired nowadays. Depression could do that to a person, she knew. And unhappiness.

What she wanted to do was to sob out her fears and tears, and all the pain her heart carried. She wanted to be held in that old remembered way, and she wanted to feel like a little girl again, warm and safe and loved. But that was impossible. Her mother was dead, and had been dead for three years. She had been killed along with Dee's father when a train was derailed and crashed into several cars that had been waiting to cross the tracks. Their car had been literally torn apart, and she had never seen them again, for the funeral had been with closed coffins. Her imagination had done terrible things, and her dreams supplied the rest. Dee had dreamt for months that their bodies had been chopped to pieces, and would wake screaming in full-throated horror. Sleeping pills had been prescribed. They had helped only a little.

The death of Charles Janson and his wife had been splashed all over national newspapers, for her father had been a millionaire several times over and his death particularly sensational. When everything had finally quieted down into a semblance of normality, Dee found herself living with her aunt and uncle in the huge house that had once seemed barely large enough to contain all the love and the laughter her family had shared. To be realistic, she couldn't miss her father as much as she missed her mother, for he had always been away on business trips and having important meetings. But he had been kind and loving when he had been home, and Dee's mother had been a ray of sunshine in the little girl's life.

Now it seemed as if the house was a great hulking empty shell.

Her father and mother had left just about everything to her, and Dee supposed vaguely that she was very, very rich, but she had no idea just how much she owned. It wasn't really hers until her eighteenth birthday anyway, and she wouldn't have full control over the estate until she was twenty-one.

But she had started to hate her money. She started to hate anything connected with her money.

Her aunt had been her mother's sister, and her aunt and uncle had been appointed as her legal guardians, for there was virtually no one else, and they had wasted no time in moving into the house as soon as the funeral was over. They didn't give a damn about her. She was very intelligent and sensitive to emotions and atmospheres, but even then Judith had made no effort to disguise what she felt. Howard, Judith's husband, was a rather weak man, and he didn't seem to mind her much, but he certainly didn't actively seek her out in any way.

Dee would never forget how Judith's mouth had

tightened and her face had whitened with rage when her parents' will had been read. The plump woman's face went suddenly sharp and pinched, in spite of her double chin. She had managed to hold on to her temper until the lawyers had left, and then she had rounded on her husband in a fury. Dee was ignored as she huddled all curled up in an armchair, her own small face white and drawn from exhaustion and grief, and incomprehension.

'Not a stinking, filthy penny!' Judith shrieked at Howard, who slid down in his chair as if to escape from the whole situation. Dee sat, stunned. 'We didn't get a stinking, lousy penny! All we get for watching the brat is an allowance!' This last was said with a sneer. 'And that gets cut off when she comes of age. We even have to submit the household books to an accountant to get the bills paid! God, I always knew my sister was tight, but I never thought she'd forget us so completely! All that money, and we get a damned pittance, while a little skinny brat of a——' She broke off suddenly, as she noticed Dee peering out from behind the chair's high winged side, eyes huge and shocked. 'Go to bed. Now!' This last was as Dee hesitated, looking from Judith to Howard. Howard averted his eyes hastily and she had been left to drag herself up to bed alone.

It had been quite devastating, to a girl of fourteen, who had just lost both her parents. She wandered around the huge house for weeks with a stunned and uncomprehending look in her large, blank blue eyes. As she slowly came out of the shock, Judith went gradually but methodically about the process of changing the house staff, letting go people who had worked for the Jansons for years and hiring people of her own choice. Eventually Dee was surrounded by complete strangers.

She had had one friend by her, though, and that was her private tutor. Until, that was, the autumn of her sixteenth year.

The exacting and excellent tutors that Dee had had over the years had been chosen with great care by her parents, and they, along with her innate, quick intelligence, had made her education leap ahead of the accepted normal rate for most teenagers. She conceived a love for learning and knowledge, and she devoured books voraciously. It was a very nice escapist tactic, to immerse oneself in an exciting and well written book. It also kept her quiet and out of Judith's way. As a result, with a ridiculous ease that had blossomed right along with her intellect, Dee was passing college entrance exams, never batting an eye.

That was why Judith and Howard decided that the best thing for everyone concerned would be to pack Dee up and send her away to college. A prestigious Eastern university had been selected, her application sent in and her things packed without further ado. Howard saw Dee to the airport and shook her hand before watching her board the plane, and that was that.

As sheltered as Dee had been, gaining her education from tutors and generally leading an isolated existence, college came as an intense, jolting shock to her system. It had been the worst year of her life.

She was too young and inexperienced, and so achingly, desperately lonely for companionship she could have died for it. Word got around that she had money, and that combined with her instinctive shyness that came across as aloofness to the other girls, along with her extreme youth, managed to keep just about everyone away from the small quiet blonde girl from Kentucky.

She got straight A's, full high marks for both terms, and was nearing a collapse when summer finally came around and she was able to go back to Kentucky. She had stopped thinking of it as home quite some time ago. It was no relief to leave school just to get back to Judith's increasing hostility and caustic comments, but the definite low point in her life was when no one remembered her birthday on May the fifteenth.

That was why, some weeks later, she was sitting in the darkness, staring off into nothing, and seriously contemplating suicide.

She crept downstairs for a sandwich later that evening, and impulsively stopped into the library to pick up a book to read. It might make her feel a little better to try and immerse herself in a makebelieve existence, one with happy endings and scary plots, or perhaps a chilling mystery to unravel and tease the mind.

It was the turning point in Dee's young life, that quick stealthy trip to the library. That was because she happened to pick up a book about a girl who had disappeared into thin air.

Her intelligence and imagination supplied the rest.

She was going to escape. She was going to make the greatest escape of all time. She was going to run away from all the unhappiness and hostility and apathy in this life and have fun, like she used to do with her mother and father. She was going to use her intelligence to work out the slyest, the sneakiest, the most devious way to ravel her trail so that no one would ever find her again. She was going to use the world as her playground instead of viewing it as the enemy to be fought. The world wasn't the enemy, people like Judith and Howard were. People who didn't know how to think for themselves, or to take risks, or to simply enjoy life with zest and enthusiasm—those were the kind of people to avoid, and she had been living in a poisoned atmosphere for years now.

Her mind suddenly active again, Dee plotted out her course of action. While she watched and waited, she paid a gas station attendant to call up the house a few times and ask for her specifically, which convinced Judith and Howard that she was actually meeting someone. She also used every opportunity she could to get away from the house, refusing to tell Judith where she had been, which was like waving a red flag under the older woman's nose. Judith ranted and raved up and down, accusing Dee of all sorts of things, of meeting someone on the sly, of going to wild parties, of whatever came to her mind. Dee sat back and listened to the various lectures, and if she didn't smile physically, she smiled in her soul.

She also wrote in deliberately childish handwriting a slightly incoherent letter of farewell to everyone, saying that she was running away with her boy-friend and that they were going to California. She sprinkled a few drops of water over the page and ended the missive on a plaintive nobody-loves-me note, signing her name in full. It took her a while; she had been trained for years to be concise and logical in her writing and to argue a point clearly and well. When she finally sealed up her farewell letter, she was chuckling irrepressibly. She'd contrived a masterpiece of nonsense!

Dee watched and waited, and the Friday she was to go to a party with Judith and Howard, she went to the bank and withdrew all her savings from her allowance, which was a tidy amount. She became suddenly very ill, actually becoming violently sick (a very difficult and painful state to achieve, she discovered, much to her own discomfort). She obviously couldn't go to the party in such a state, so the housekeeper was to keep an eye on her while Judith and Howard went. Dee had the evening to herself. She waited until her aunt and uncle were actually gone and then got to work, trailing around in her huge bedroom in her nightgown and ready to pop back into bed in case the housekeeper should check on her. She packed a small canvas bag of things she couldn't bear to leave, along with a few clothing essentials, and called the airport to book two flights if any were open on an evening flight to

California, to confuse the issue. It would be one more indication that she was running away with someone else. Of course she had no intention of being on the flight.

The one place in the entire state of Kentucky where no one would ever think to look for her was in her own bedroom, and in Deirdre's room was both a walk-in closet and a private bath. The house was not only very large but also very old, and Dee had lived in that room all her life. She knew it intimately, and she was especially familiar with the small square opening in the roof of her closet. It led to a tiny cubbyhole that was in the attic but was sealed off from the larger open space by a crosswork of beams, rendering that corner of the attic invisible. A loose board painted the same colour as her closet lay over the square, panelled hole. It had been her favourite hiding place as a child and her mother might have eventually thought to look there for her, but she knew that neither Judith nor the relatively new servants knew of its existence. Even if they thought to check it, they would assume that it led to the attic, and they would look there. She could sit on the board if anyone actually pressed a curious finger at it.

She pushed the board aside and hauled up everything that she was going to take with her, plus a canister of water and food stolen from the kitchen. She also went down to the library and picked out several paperbacks, leisurely unlocking the front door as she went. Back in her room she made up her bed to look as if she were still in it, propped her farewell letter on the dressing table in front of her mirror, and shoved the books along with a powerful flashlight and extra batteries up into the hole.

She then jumped into swift action, tearing out of her nightdress and yanking on sturdy clothes, fearful of being discovered. Then, to assure herself of an escape route, she climbed out of her window and slid down the branch of the nearby oak tree. No limbs broke and she didn't break her own neck, so if it worked the first time, it would work again. She stole in by the front door, locked it behind her, and stole back upstairs. She was ready to escape.

Uncontrollable giggles assailed her as she attempted to negotiate the cramped opening with extreme difficulty. It had never been this tight of a squeeze, but then she had been smaller before, and hadn't so much packed in the hole. She really had to struggle, slight as she was, to get her hips through the tiny opening, and rather doubted that anyone else would believe that anyone but a slight child could fit through. She found that she was enjoying herself immensely in a way that she hadn't for years, and the happy excitement, the thrill of adventure, and the just plain mischievousness of it all was exhilarating.

The uproar of the house the next morning, when she was found missing, was quite entertaining. She munched through a breakfast of apples as she listened to everything, holding a hand over her mouth to keep from laughing aloud at her aunt and uncle's reaction. They were stupefied, incredulous, and Judith was absolutely furious. Dee heard herself called some names that she'd never heard before, and that was sobering, but she was soon seeing the humour of the situation, since her aunt's opinion of her didn't matter in the slightest. The noise in her room was quite racketing, and she heard several conversations between the police and members of the household. Everyone agreed that the house should be searched, and a few people came up to the attic to shine a few flashlights into corners, but as everyone wholeheartedly believed that she was gone, it was a half-hearted effort, and she relaxed afterwards.

When three in the morning rolled around, she slipped out of her hole and used the bathroom quickly, refilling her water supply stealthily, heart pounding and ears tuned. No one was up, though, and she made it back to her hiding place uncaught.

The next day was sheer torture for her, cramped in such a confining way and unable to make a sound. She began to understand just what the Jews must have gone through when they had been forced into hiding during Hitler's regime. She was bored, very stiff, and aching all over. The day crept by agonisingly until in the late afternoon she heard sounds coming from below that made her stiffen.

Footsteps entered her room. Someone had left the closet door open earlier that day and she could hear everything quite clearly. Judith was speaking. 'I'm so glad you were available, Mr Carridine. Yes, this is her room. Everything is just about how we found it, even the bed.'

A deep, masculine voice answered her. 'Where's the letter that she left? May I see it, please? . . . Thank you.' There was silence for a few moments while he apparently perused the contents of the missive, and when he spoke again his voice was overtly polite but with undertones of sarcasm that Dee caught, even through a layer of wood. 'Mrs Kimble, does this letter strike you at all as being odd?'

Dee sat up straight in the darkness and pricked up her ears. She had met Mike Carridine only once before, and that had been a few years ago, when he had been hired to find a missing document for her guardians. He had been quick, methodical, and highly intelligent, and she remembered vividly what he looked like. He was big, very big. He also had a way of looking right through a person as if he could tell what they were thinking by staring into their eyes. She somehow had thought he could, too, and she cursed her luck at having someone like him on her trail. She had the impression that he would be a formidable opponent and she didn't want to cross wits with him.

Judith was answering, 'Why, I don't know what you mean.'

His low, pleasant voice replied, 'How old is Deirdre?'

There was a silence as Judith hesitated, and then, 'Seventeen, I believe. Yes, she is seventeen.'

'Her own guardian isn't sure?' Dee could imagine him with his eyes sardonic and one eyebrow cocked. She had seen him do that once, those years before, and it had made quite an impression on her. 'Doesn't it strike you as being odd, Mrs Kimble, that a highly intelligent girl who had just made straight A's at one of the most demanding and prestigious universities in the country would write such a pack of nonsense?'

'I'd never thought of it before.' Judith was sounding flustered. Footsteps sounded as if someone were pacing the room.

'Apparently, Mrs Kimble, there's a lot that you don't know about your ward, including her age. Could I perhaps see the downstairs, do you think...?' The voices gradually faded away into silence, while Dee chewed her lip thoughtfully. This was going to be harder than she'd first imagined.

She slipped away in the middle of the night and eventually managed to hitch a ride with a cheerful truck driver who shouted a breezy conversation over the engine's roar all the way to Virginia. When they had stopped for a few minutes, she called a major newspaper and told them that a millionaire heiress was missing, and that she couldn't reveal her name since she was an employee at the house and might lose her job. It was a dirty trick, but it would hamper Carridine's movements, and she had a feeling she'd need all the help she could get.

CHAPTER TWO

In the end, Dee remembered wryly, she had cravenly slipped away from the trucker while he was occupied with something else, leaving a brief, apologetic note behind. Then she had opened up a bank account with a hundred dollars and her real name at a well known bank, and she had left that city on an interstate bus wearing a brown wig that same day. She had figured that it would take a while to unravel everything, especially the bank account, for why would anyone just set up an account and leave good money untouched? To buy time, of course, but she had hoped that it wouldn't be so obvious to someone trying to figure out what she was up to. Then she had zigzagged across the country, hitting only very large cities and never staying long, until finally she had ended up in Akron, Ohio, exhausted, discouraged, and low on funds.

It had only been the beginning of the struggle, she was to find out. She then had to find a job and a place to live that was both affordable and safe. For two weeks straight she spent every day, all day, out looking for a job, any kind of job. She applied at stores, restaurants, any business she could think of, and nobody seemed to be hiring. Finally, when Sammy had interviewed her for a waitressing position and had told her that he would get in touch later, she had replied quietly, 'I would rather you told me yes or no right now, sir. I've been looking all over for a job and I'm gone all day long, so you couldn't get in touch with me. It seems a pity to waste your time and raise my hopes if you aren't really considering me for the job.'

Sammy had taken one startled look at her face, and

had seen the quiet desperation and hopelessness. She had started work the next day.

Yes, she had grown up a lot in the last nine months. She could be responsible for herself. She had been a seventeen-year-old girl when she had run away from home, and now she was a young woman. And a stranger wanted to take her freedom away from her.

The phone shrilled a double ring and she went to answer. It occurred to her that this would be a good, easy way to find out if she was at home or not, but she had an unlisted number and by the time she'd thought of it the receiver was off the hook and the damage done. She sighed, 'Hello.'

'Hi, kid,' Kim answered cheerily. 'The big bad, nasty man is gone now. He said something about going to the local hospitals, so I'd say you're safe for a little while. You didn't wreck my car, did you?'

'Of course not,' Dee answered absently, thinking hard.

'Too bad, sugar. I could use the insurance money—who cares about the car, it's a health hazard, anyway! Well, I need to run, a table has just been seated in my section. See you!'

Replacing the receiver, Dee wandered back to packing. She didn't have much time before her cab would be here. Picking up her knapsack and stuffing her handbag inside, she went into the bathroom to get some personal items. Nobody could be sure of what Carridine would really do, and it was a gamble to assume that he had gone to the hospitals, but she had no choice. She couldn't afford to waste any time, that was for sure.

A crunching of gravel sounded outside, and she froze. It couldn't be! It had to be the cab coming early. She ran out to her bedroom window and looked out—and nearly fell from shock. Mike Carridine was opening up the car door and getting out. How in the world did he know to come here? she asked herself frantically as she swept through the apartment, closing her suitcase and shoving it back into the closet. He would be inside any moment now—what should she do?

She sank slowly on to the couch, her hands idle and her face calm enough, though her thoughts were churning chaotically. There was nothing she could do but meet him. Mrs Gordon would tell him that she was home, so there could be no pretence on that score. For the time being, she was neatly trapped.

She went into the kitchen to start some coffee. Soon the pungent smell was filling the tiny apartment and she stood indecisively in the minuscule cooking area, hands clasped nervously. No, there wasn't any use in pretending to herself: she was very apprehensive about meeting the man who had been able to track her thus far. She had become used to thinking of him as the enemy, the pursuer, the stalker bent on his prey, and the imagery was now frightening to contemplate.

What would he be like? she asked herself. She couldn't really remember anything about his personality, though his physical presence had impressed her, years ago. Would he be a thug? She wouldn't put it past Judith to hire one, but no, that didn't fit in with what she knew of him. One thing she could be sure of was that he wouldn't be easy to fool.

Heavy footsteps sounded on the stairway, and she tensed. They were very deliberate and unhesitating. She had herself so keyed up that when the quick, hard knock sounded on her door, even though she had been expecting it, she jumped violently. This wouldn't do, she scolded herself. If you aren't feeling poised, then act it, stupid. With that tender admonition to herself, she took a quick look in the mirror at herself.

The last of the adolescent plumpness had disappeared in the past nine months, leaving her still small but more slim in tight jeans and a black sweater. Her blonde hair could use a comb, she saw fleetingly, but then it always could. Her vivid blue eyes were even more huge than ever in a naturally pale face. This impression was created by delicate bone structure and high thin cheekbones. There was a thinness about her face and body that had become apparent as she had matured. She had often thought she might have been a cat in a former life, for her entire body was built along a slim, streamlined grace that was reminiscent of a cat's lithe fragility, or perhaps a greyhound's raciness. The impression was not a mere illusion: she could run very swiftly and well, having a natural aptitude for speed.

She was not taking time to stand and contemplate all this, however, for that firm knock sounded again at her door, and she went to answer.

The door swung slowly open, and her eyes looked up to meet those of Mike Carridine. She received a slight jolt, for she hadn't remembered the colour of his eyes and found herself looking into jewel-green eyes, arresting in the man's brown face. He was large, with masculinely wide shoulders encased in a light spring jacket over a grey shirt that was casually open at the throat. He had on a pair of black slacks that looked to be well fitting and yet comfortable. His frame, she noticed, as she ran assessing eyes over him, was not as bulky as she remembered but instead more on the slim side, though well muscled. Of course, she acknowledged fleetingly, she was remembering with the eyes of a child. His dark hair was ruffled from the March wind.

She finished her perusal and looked up, only then realising that he had been looking her over too. It was not a sexual look or crude: they both had been sizing each other up as opponents, assessingly and objectively. 'Mr Carridine,' she said quietly, holding out a slim hand. It seemed to startle him, for his eyebrows shot up as he took her proffered hand and shook it briefly. She felt the latent strength in his grip as he held her small hand carefully and then let go.

'Miss Janson. May I come in?' was his pleasantly smooth reply. She inclined her head and stepped back, and he paced into her living room. It seemed suddenly smaller than ever, and she felt restricted.

'I've made us coffee,' she offered politely. 'Would you like a cup? But I was forgetting—you had coffee at Dandy's, didn't you?'

After a quick, cursory glance around at the cheerful atmosphere of the small room and the homey decorations on the walls, he had brought his gaze back to her and was watching her with a disturbing closeness. 'Yes, but it was only one cup. Another would be nice, thank you.'

'You're welcome,' she answered automatically. 'Have a seat and I'll pour us some.' She walked into the kitchen space, feeling a little better as the intervening wall hid her from his steady, alert gaze. She called out, 'What do you take in yours?'

'Nothing, thank you.' That voice was really pleasant, she thought idly, spooning sugar and milk into her cup. The humour of the situation had her smiling wryly as she came back into the living room space with the two carefully balanced mugs. Her sparkling, amused eyes met his and she received another jolt, though she couldn't explain why. 'A good joke?' he enquired politely, taking the cup from her.

'I suppose so,' she murmured, then broke through her reserve and told him frankly. 'Isn't this a rich scene? I've done my best to shake you loose from my trail, and for nine months we've been in opposition with each other, and here we are, face to face for the first time, politely drinking coffee and acting civilised.'

'You see me as being your opponent, then?' he queried curiously, cocking an eyebrow while sipping from his cup. Dee was very aware of that green, keen gaze, and she dropped her eyes to his hands.

'Yes,' she replied shortly. 'Opponents matching wits—yes, I'd say so.' She set her cup down without tasting it and studied her fingernails carefully. They needed attention, for they were getting a bit too long for comfort at work.

Tense silence. Then, 'You were unsurprised when you answered the door just now,' he commented, and the comment was a question. He leaned back in the only chair in the room, stretching out his long legs. They reached nearly to where she sat, and she transferred her gaze to one shoe for a moment's perusal before answering.

There was no reason to lie. 'I was working today and saw you. But then you know that from talking to Kim, don't you? She called me when you left the restaurant, but I wasn't sure that you would be right here.' Her lips twisted. 'I was gambling that you weren't coming here right away.'

'Ah, yes,' he answered mildly. 'The hospital gambit. It was a good try for a last-minute effort, Deirdre. May I call you that? I've been looking for you so long, I feel I know you.'

Her head came around to his face and she found him smiling slightly. Her eyes narrowed at that. He looked complacent, well in control of the situation, in charge. In charge of her? Like hell, she thought grimly. It would be worth it to see his face when he found her gone, soon. It did not pay to become too complacent. The only problem was, she didn't know how she was going to get out of this one. 'Call me Dee,' she offered casually, widening her eyes and smiling at him, friendly.

That sharp green gaze flickered over her again. 'And of course my first name is Mike. Your landlady told me you were sick. Is it really true, or were you just being consistent with your story?'

'I'm not feeling well,' she said ruefully, 'but I think it's more from nerves than anything else. I'd begun to relax a bit, you see, and seeing you get out of your car this afternoon gave me a jolt.' When she had answered the door a few minutes ago, she had been very pale from apprehension. 'Tell me, how did you know to check here? Kim surely didn't let the cat out of the bag, did she? I thought she was a better liar than that.'

'It was an educated hunch. You see, I'd guessed from a very strange conversation that I overheard when— Kim, is it?—answered the restaurant's phone. She jotted down a number and promised the party that she'd call back. I got a look at the number that she had put down and called from a pay phone, finding that it was a local time and temperature recording. Nothing conclusive,' he ended dryly, 'but enough to make me wonder, and it couldn't hurt to check here before checking the hospitals. I'm beginning to recognise your methods.'

She acknowledged that with a nod, her eyelids down to hide their expression. She was thinking rapidly, furiously, and for the first time since she had seen him getting out of his car, hopefully. Her knapsack and bag were in the bathroom, and there was a window. Could she pretend sickness or something, and get in there to try to get out? The problem was that it was a second story window and she had no idea if there was anything to climb down, or that she would even fit through the tiny square. It was, however, worth considering.

She needed a little time to think, so she sat back and looked at him directly, her blue eyes losing their friendly light. 'So,' she said abruptly, 'now what? Surely you had something in mind for this occasion?'

A quick turn of his head had him looking at her oddly. 'I'm going to take you back home, of course,' he stated calmly. The confidence in his manner made her hackles rise, but she managed to hide her antipathy for the moment as she stared at him unblinkingly, eyes wide. His expression changed, became more gentle. 'There are some very worried people back in Kentucky,

Dee. They care about you and want you back home. Surely you can work things out, now that everyone's had plenty of time to think?'

'Don't make me laugh!' she snarled, and as quickly as her hostility had surfaced, it vanished, as she got a grim hold on herself. She had time to notice that his brows had shot down at her outburst, his eyes becoming sharper, stern. She continued hardly, 'Do you happen to know the law in Ohio, Mr Carridine?' She saw him register her deliberate use of his last name, felt him tense. 'I don't. In some states it's against the law to try to force a minor over sixteen years of age to go back home. Don't you think you'd better check up on that before you so blithely decide your course of action?'

'I don't need to,' he said quietly, his eyes now as hard as hers, implacable, frightening. He really was the enemy, she thought, sickened. He was as much the enemy as all the others. 'You see,' he said gently, the tone making her shudder, 'you're going to come with me, or I'm going to the newspapers and tell them your name, address, place of work and real identity. It's one or the other, Deirdre. Your choice.'

'God!' she muttered, paling. Her eyes searched his and found him absolutely sincere, with no softening of resolve. He didn't exactly look cruel, she had to admit. He was merely doing his job, no matter what. 'Why? Why does it have to be that way? Why can't I just go on with my life as it is here? *Damn* it, man, it's my life, not yours or anybody else's!'

'You should go back if for no other reason than your obligations,' he said sternly. 'I was hired to find you. If you don't wish to accompany me back, I can easily call your aunt and uncle to fly out and make the trip back with you, if you'd like. It doesn't matter to me. I've done my job.'

Dee had blanched at the mention of her aunt and uncle and he had seen it. His face had changed, grown

puzzled, but he didn't press the issue. He let silence fall
in the room as he gave her time to consider the options
he had given her. She was feeling that terrible sense of
being trapped again, and it was stronger than before.
She couldn't go back! That would be the death of all
her independence and happiness. Judith and Howard
were her legal guardians until her twenty-first birthday,
and that was an eternity away. For all Dee's blossoming
maturity, she somehow shrank at the thought of
confronting her aunt again. She couldn't, wouldn't do
it. She had a right to her own life, and this man sitting
so quietly in front of her now was doing his best to take
away that right.

'I don't understand,' she muttered sickly. 'I really
don't comprehend this. I'm nearly eighteen years old!
This is a ridiculous situation!'

'You may be nearly eighteen, but you aren't like
other eighteen-year-olds,' he replied, impatience creep-
ing into his inflections. 'Good God, child, can you
imagine the horror if some nut or criminal found out
that you were living in a cheap, accessible apartment in
the bad part of Akron, Ohio? I wouldn't give two dimes
for your chances of survival!'

'Who would know, if nobody told them?' she cried
out, then put a shaking hand to her forehead and then
to her mouth. She closed her eyes and swallowed hard.
One part of her was acknowledging wryly that it wasn't
wholly assumed. This man was overwhelming her.

'Are you all right?' he asked her sharply, leaning
forward to stare into her face.

'I'll be fine,' she mumbled into her hand, too quickly.
She bent her head and stared at the worn carpet, letting
all her anxiety, her misery show. She didn't have to act
that. 'W-would you excuse me for a moment? I'm a bit
nauseated . . .'

He rose to his feet when she did, his eyes following
her out of the room, his expression thoughtful and

concerned. She left, mentally cursing. She hadn't wanted to see that concern. It didn't support the impression that she had carried of him all these months. She didn't want to know if he could be kind.

She closed the bathroom door behind her and carefully, silently locked it, then she flew to the window to assess the situation. It looked extremely difficult, but possible. There was a drainpipe right along the edge of her window and if it would hold her weight, then she could shin down. It was an old pipe, and made out of sturdy metal, not like the newer, lighter ones. She would take the risk. Moving rapidly, she switched on the bathroom sink taps so that the water was gushing out at full strength, then she carefully slid open the ancient window. It creaked and she hissed with frustration, but she didn't really think that Carridine could have heard it over the water.

The window stopped moving upwards and she wasn't sure if she could fit through, but she was in too much of a hurry to struggle with it. She zipped up her knapsack and threw it out of the window, then grasped the edge of the sink with her hands for support while she struggled to get her legs out of the window. It was a furious, quick, frantic wriggling squeeze to get her hips through, but she made it and slid with a bump to hang with her shoulders in and her bottom out. She had lost the grip on the sink as she had scooted back, and she scrambbled for a handhold on the windowsill before edging one shoulder and then the other out the tiny open area. Then, hanging by her hands from the second story window and suddenly realising that if she fell she would be landing on harsh, cutting gravel, she cautiously tried to reach for the drainpipe with one hand while calling herself a crazy fool for even attempting the stunt. She barely reached the pipe, but was able to get a firm enough grip, and there she hung, unable to loosen either hand for fear of losing her grip entirely and falling. She closed her eyes, gritted her teeth so hard it hurt her jaw, and with a supreme effort unclenched her right hand.

The world swung around frighteningly and the strain on her left arm was enough to make her cry out, but she was soon latching on to the drain with her right hand like a hook of steel, then she was going down, hand over hand, until the ground was at a reasonable distance for dropping. She let go with both hands, landed at a crouch, turned and picked up her knapsack, and was out into the street with a huge spring.

The whole manoeuvre had taken perhaps a minute and a half.

She saw a yellow battered car bearing a taxi emblem on its hood turning on to her street, down the block, and she could have laughed at the wonderful timing. It was the first thing that had gone right that day. She raced down the street, confident that Carridine couldn't see her as her living room window was on the opposite side of the house, her bathroom window being towards the back. At her frantic wave, the taxi slewed over to stop beside her. She briefly looked over her shoulder, then she was opening the back door of the car and saying breathlessly, 'Thank God you're here! I told you the wrong time, and I might miss my plane! Could you step on it, please, and get me to the Municipal Airport as fast as you can haul it?'

'Sure enough, sweet thing,' the cabby said, winking. He was a heavy, good-natured man who looked to be in his forties or so. He cheerfully stamped on the gas pedal and the car shot forward with a jerk that sent Dee back into her seat. She squeaked and ducked down as the taxi shot by Mrs Gordon's house. She sincerely hoped that Carridine hadn't been looking out of the window. Everything had happened so incredibly fast, though, he was probably still standing worriedly at the bathroom door. If he was suspicious, he would surely be knocking and calling to her instead of gazing outside, so she rather thought she was safe. Still she couldn't assume it, and would have to go on the hunch that he had seen the taxi. When he found her gone, he would be able to put two and two together, but he still wouldn't know where she had gone. She estimated that she had a fifteen-minute lead, if that.

And she was feeling pretty desperate.

As the cab driver pulled to the kerb just outside the airport building, Dee stuffed a bill into his hand and told him shortly to keep the change, and she was out of the car and into the building before he had finished his thanks. Once inside, she took stock to the right and then to the left, and she caught sight of a flight plan posted to the left. Running over, she sent a quick eye down the flights. The next one would be leaving in half an hour, and it was an airline she wasn't familiar with. She got quick directions from a girl in a nearby candy shop, then she was rushing through the huge open walkway, passing slower people and elbowing her way around standing groups. Her heart was thumping madly from her swift pace and from the sheer exhilaration of being on the run again, using her wits, dodging discovery. Adrenalin was sluicing through her. She could feel it in her heightened awareness, the swift ticking of her brain.

Catching sight of the airline's counter, she ran over. 'Could you tell me if there's an empty seat by any chance on your flight to Washington D.C. in a half an hour?' she asked breathlessly, thinking, what the hell? I've always wanted to go there. The girl at the counter frowned.

'I don't really know,' she replied, glancing through some things behind the counter. 'The list isn't here. Let me go and get someone who can find out for you.' She disappeared in the back while Dee concentrated on getting her breathing steady, looking cautiously around her.

It was just plain luck that she saw Carridine before he saw her. He entered the building with long, impatient strides, looking around him, eyes darting alertly to his right, and Dee was to his left. 'Oh, my God!' she moaned, clutching her hair with both hands in furious exasperation. 'How the hell does he do it—radar?' And she ducked behind a group of several businessmen, wondering what she was going to do next. She edged around a corner and found herself looking at rows of lockers for hire, and then she looked at her knapsack. What she needed desperately at the moment was mobilisation and anonymity. She rushed over to the counter and rented a locker space, throwing her things in it quickly after a mad scramble for her money and identification, which she stuffed into her pocket. Then she slammed the door shut, thrust the key into her pocket as well, turned and muffled a shriek. At a distance, over several people's heads, Carridine was searching the area, and his eyes lit on her. Then with a distinctly ominous frown that she personally didn't care for one bit, he started to shoulder his way towards her.

That one sight was all she needed. She whirled and ran. She had the advantage as she dodged, ducked under arms, and darted through the people. The airport was very busy that day, and she was smaller than Carridine, more able to squeeze past people and duck around obstacles. At least she thought that she had the advantage over Carridine, but when she darted her head around for a quick look behind her, she saw that he was quite definitely gaining on her.

There was nothing else for it. She bent her head, clenched her hands into fists, and burst into a quick-footed, agile sprint that made her previous pace look as if she'd been standing still. People turned, looked and pointed at the two running through the airport and any other time Dee might have been embarrassed, but at the moment she had something else on her mind. And she could run. She regulated her breathing, concentrated on nothing but the rhythm of her speed and the path before her, and ran as if she were racing the hundred-yard dash, putting everything she had into it. Just in front of her a worker pushed a cart of luggage right into her way and, being too close to slow down and stop or to try and avoid it, she merely increased her speed, lengthened her stride, and picked up her feet at the appropriate moment. She sailed right over. Then she swerved abruptly to her left, ran through the double glass doors, and picked up her speed again until she was running at maximum strength.

After a moment she risked a quick glance behind her to see if she had by any chance lost Carridine when she had ducked out of the door, and she saw him, even closer this time and still determinedly sprinting after her. She turned, her breath coming in huge, controlled gasps, and stubbornly fixed her mind on running still faster, then she reached down inside her somewhere, called for a little more speed, a little more energy, and her body gave it to her. She actually increased her speed, still sprinting full out and punishing her body dreadfully as she pelted down the sidewalk. It was more than a quarter of a mile now, easily, from the airport.

She couldn't believe it. She was a daily jogger, in excellent shape, and she was a talented runner. She could race at high speeds for incredible distances, and few men could even keep up with her, and yet he was actually gaining on her! That man was good. The only thing she could hope for, short of a twisted ankle, was that he would burn himself out before she in such a bruising sprint. Most short-distance runners could pick up incredible speed, but they tended to burn out quickly. They couldn't keep the pace up. She could only hope that he was not in as good condition as she was.

She could hear the footsteps pelting on the sidewalk behind her and somehow, teeth gritted and face grimacing, she managed to step her pace again, slightly. Her breath was coming in great starving gasps, and with every heave red-hot molten fire bolted through her lungs. Her blood pumped painfully at her temples, and at the back of her eyes. Piercing throbs were shooting through her head as her body protested against this punishment, and she wondered, as she heard the closing footsteps and Mike's harsh, laboured breathing just behind her, which would break first, her body or her mind.

And just then something was flung like a bolas around her two slim legs, and she came down heavily on the sidewalk, the breath knocked cruelly out of her. She doubled up, gasping for air, her arms wrapped around her sides, and Carridine let go of her legs to lie beside her, panting as heavily as she, his lips pulled back to reveal white, gritted teeth. He pulled himself to his knees, wide chest heaving, and rested a moment.

'Damn, you're fast!' she heard him say, shaking his head and drawing one hand across his brow. His dark hair was windblown and tangled, she saw, and one shaking hand went to her own. Her eyes had slewed to him when he spoke, but she was still fighting too hard to get her breath back to respond. 'But you weren't good enough, sweetheart. All the same, it was a hell of a try.' He stood and reached down a big, supportive hand, and she crouched for a moment, just looking her fury and hate at him. He merely looked indifferent, and she slowly reached out and grasped his hand with her own.

He gave a great heave and helped her to her feet and, with a sudden swiftness that was like a striking adder, belying the bruising and exhausting race she'd just run, Dee came out of her crouch with the full force of her moving body and the power of her rage, and planted a crippling right hook hard on Carridine's jaw.

CHAPTER THREE

SUDDENLY horrified, she watched his head snap back with the force of her blow, and he took an involuntary step backwards, for balance. Then, his head coming down and his jewel-green eyes leaping with fury, he jerked out his right foot and knocked her legs out from under her. Dee went down like a sack of potatoes, hard on her hip, landing with a panting grunt.

They were both totally oblivious to the passers by who were watching avidly, curiously, staring and pointing. Dee curled up on herself on the sidewalk, wincing from the pain of her fall and rubbing at her bruised hip. She just went inward into her misery, anger and outrage, and, yes, fear. She didn't try to get up or move; she just sat on the pavement with her head bent and cried.

Somewhere above her head she heard an impatient-sounding, gusty sigh, then two gentle hands came under her arms and lifted her right up off the sidewalk and deposited her on her feet. Then, as she refused to look up from under her curtaining fall of bright hair, she felt a strong, heavy arm circle her slender shoulders and steer her around the way they had come. They walked this way for the half a mile or so back to the airport's parking lot, in silence, close together. Dee didn't really know why she didn't object to his arm around her, especially when he was definitely the enemy in her eyes, and a great personal threat to her way of life. All she knew was that her defiance and anger had crumbled and she was succumbing to the need for personal support and human contact, something she had been denied for too long.

Back by his dark green sedan car, Carridine asked her suddenly, the sound making her jump, 'I saw you by the storage lockers. Were you putting something in one that you'd like to retrieve before we go?'

She nodded, keeping her face averted. They then walked inside and she got her knapsack, doing her best to ignore the stares of people. They left, and as she climbed silently into his car, he asked her quietly, 'Would you like to go back to your apartment? It's a little late in the day to do much of anything else, I'm afraid.'

She nodded again, biting her lip and staring out her window. There was a moment of stillness, and she could feel his regard, but she still couldn't turn to look at him. She was too afraid that she'd burst into tears again, and she didn't want to feel humiliated any more than she already did. Finally he started the car and eased out of his parking space, and she found the courage to speak. 'I lost my temper. I'm sorry for hitting you.'

She nearly jumped out of her skin when a firmhand came down on her jeans-clad knee, squeezing briefly before returning to the steering wheel. 'I don't blame you, child,' he replied mildly. 'I would have felt like doing the same, I guess. I'm sorry for knocking you down. Are we even?'

Dee stole a quick look at his profile as he turned out on to a street, and though his brows were lowered, he was smiling slightly as he cast her a sidelong glance. Then memory returned and realisation hit her, and she withdrew to her side of the car, as far as she could go, saying tightly, 'Not quite.'

His smile disappeared and his expression became remote. He nodded curtly and commented. 'Fair enough.' And for the rest of the drive back to her apartment, he concentrated frowningly on the road.

They managed to miss Mrs Gordon as they went up the stairs to her tiny apartment, and after entering, Dee

turned and asked him politely, 'Would you like to hav
supper now? I was planning on having hamburger
tonight and I'm afraid ground beef is the only meat
have unfrozen. We could have meat loaf, if that woul
suit you better.' Her blue eyes as she looked at him wer
expressionless, blank. She was doing her hardest t
keep her expression schooled into that blanknes
because inside she was still teeming with waves of rag
and resentment at this man who had the power to upse
her life so completely. She wouldn't let him see i
though. She'd already shown too much. Her eye
travelled to his left jawline, as she thought of her blow
and she was inwardly satisfied to see that there was ;
slight mark there.

Mike was leaning against the doorpost, his green gaz
narrowed on her face, his brows lowered as if i
puzzlement. 'Hamburgers would be fine,' he said
slowly, considering her closely. 'But if you would
prefer, we could go out to eat. There's no need for you
to cook something here, if you'd rather not.'

Her expression never changed. She just regarded him
as emotionlessly as if he were the refrigerator, and said,
'I'd rather not eat out, thank you. Not only do I get my
fill of restaurants at work, but I really don't have the
money to spend.' She turned around and pulled out the
meat, pleased with her slight dig at him.

She couldn't see his face, but she could tell from his
tone of voice that he was displeased with what she had
said as he replied briefly, 'I would of course pay for
your meal, since it was my invitation.'

The anger inside her flickered up again, and she
turned to stare at him coldly. 'And would you mark it
down as expenses? But of course you would, and
eventually it would be my money that would pay for my
meal, wouldn't it? It's ironic, isn't it, that my money is
paying your fees to find me, when it's the last thing in
the world I personally want?'

His face tightened into a dark anger, but he obviously made an effort to control himself as he said quietly, 'But it's your aunt and uncle who are paying my wages, not you, so I believe this conversation is irrelevant.' And his expression was cold, repelling, but something hurt and angry inside of her made her retaliate.

'My dear sir,' she drawled nastily, her eyes supremely bitter, 'who the hell do you think supports my aunt and uncle? Good old Howard hasn't worked in at least five years.'

He had begun to turn away, but at that he swivelled sharply back, his face wearing a look of frowning disbelief. 'Do you mean to tell me that your money is supporting your guardians?'

Her insolent pose dropped suddenly and her eyes fell away as she turned back to the hamburger and the stove. She reached out an absent hand and switched on a burner, her head bowed and shoulders hunched. She had no idea how young and vulnerable she looked at that moment, as if the cares of the world were residing on her shoulders alone. He stared at her as if he couldn't look away. 'They're living in my house,' she said simply, as if that explained everything. 'I used to love that big old lovely home.' Her eyes stared unseeingly at the drab wallpaper behind the stove as her nimble fingers shaped a meat patty. She shook herself briefly, and glanced at him leaning down against the cracked sink. He was very near, with his shoulder nearly touching hers, and his arms were folded across his chest. He was regarding her intently and she saw concern again.

Her eyes went carefully blank and her lips smiled. 'Would you like one hamberger or two?' she asked him politely.

'Two, please. Dee, didn't you have anyone to talk to, back home, to go to for help? Wasn't there anyone you could have turned to, instead of running away?'

Her mouth twisted and it was an ugly sight. 'Do yo want to watch the evening news? I think it's time, if yo would turn on the television.' She didn't look at him slamming that door she had so briefly opened wit everything inside her. 'I like to listen to it while I fix m supper.'

Silence, no movement. Then a strangely weary sigh 'The news would be nice. Perhaps after supper w could——'

She said with a chatty deliberation, interrupting whatever he'd been ready to suggest, 'There's a good movie on tonight and I've been wanting to see it. I missed it at the movie theatres. We can watch it, since we aren' leaving tonight after all.' She flipped the grilling burgers deftly, then she put vegetables on to cook. 'Where in the world are you going to sleep? I don't suppose you would trust me to stay quietly in my bed tonight?'

'No,' she was assured with a hard amusement. 'That's the last thing I'd expect from you. I'll just bunk down on the floor by the bed, I think. It'll save you money if we don't stay at a motel tonight.' That last was said sarcastically, and she knew that her dig about paying his wages had hit a nerve. While she finished supper, he went to the living room and used her phone, and over the noises she was making, she heard him address her aunt directly. Her appetite was completely gone by the time the meal was finished.

After their simple meal, she made coffee and they sat on her bed and watched the movie. It was very good and so funny that she sometimes had to hold her sides from laughing so much. Once her merry blue eyes travelled to Mike's large frame beside her, and she caught him watching her instead of the television, his gaze cloudy and troubled. Her smile died as she was shocked into the awareness of the situation, amazed at how she tended to forget. She shrank back, and the rest of the movie was spent in unsmiling silence.

As she was putting away the dishes after they had drained dry, much later, she opened and closed the few cupboards that she had over the stove, shuffling things around. It was a real effort to get everything to fit into the small space she had for storage, and the cupboards not only held all of her dishware, but her canned goods and spices, along with everything that should have gone in the medicine cabinet, if she had had one. She impatiently thrust aside the aspirin and a small pill bottle that held only a few more pills, as she put away the salt and pepper shaker—then she stopped dead, heart thumping madly and throat constricting, staring at that little, nearly empty medicine bottle.

Then her gaze swivelled to the closed bathroom door where Mike was washing up, her eyes wide and horrified at the audacity of the thought that had struck her. The bottle held prescription sleeping pills, left over from several months ago when the vivid, horrifying nightmare of her parents' deaths had resurfaced because of the stress she had been under to find a job and a place to live before her money ran out. She hadn't wanted to throw away the leftover pills in case the nightmare returned. She stared at that little white bottle, her blue eyes narrowed and catlike, then her eyes flew to the closed bathroom door again, from which she could hear water running and the sounds of him moving around. It would be a terrible thing to do, but she was going to try.

She wondered if she could pull it off.

When Mike emerged a few minutes later, he found her spooning in fresh coffee grounds into a paper liner in her coffee-maker. He came and peered over her shoulder for a moment, and she said briefly, 'Getting it ready for breakfast in the morning,' and held her breath. Her hands were steady, though, as she slid the container into place on the machine, and since he had said nothing, she turned to face him.

And she received a shock. The actual reality of him sleeping in the same room with her had not really surfaced into her busy thoughts until then, and she stared at him with wide eyes. He had on a light pair of cotton pyjama bottoms and absolutely nothing else, his brown smooth muscled chest bare, as were his feet. Her eyes bounced down him and then away. His were trained on her face and he murmured amusedly, 'Be thankful I've made the concession of wearing the bottoms. I usually wear nothing.'

Dee didn't say anything. What was there to say? With an effort, she tore her gaze away from that bare, surprisingly attractive chest and walked determinedly over to her closet, drawing out two blankets and throwing them at him. He caught them deftly. 'That's all I have,' she said quickly. 'You'll have to make do with those.'

'I'll be fine.' He squatted down and began to lay them out, and for the life of her she couldn't keep from staring at the smooth, graceful lines of his body clearly revealed. The line of his powerful back curved down to the leanness of his slim hips, and both legs looked underneath the thin cloth to be well shaped, muscular. She knew from experience how powerful those legs were. If he had been anywhere near her, she knew she would never have had a prayer of outrunning him, let alone getting as far as she did. He was so very quick, and that was a lot of motive power, moving such bulk so swiftly. She turned again, jerkily, and grabbed her own night clothes from her nearby dresser, heading for the bathroom with a muffled, 'Excuse me.' He had to stand to let her past.

In the privacy of the bathroom, she viciously brushed her small teeth as she mentally cursed her wide eyes and nervous thumping heart. Sure, she had no experience with living closely with a man, and she had been sheltered during her upbringing and had rarely made friends with the opposite sex, but that didn't account for the wild pounding of her heart and the acute awareness that she was feeling for this man. He was obviously a mature, fully grown male, and an attractive one at that, and that was all. She could control herself better, she knew she could. There was nothing special about this man. There was nothing special at all.

Except for the fact that he was the most intelligent, intuitive, capable man she had ever met. There were few people that Dee actually felt intimidated by, but he was one of them, for he could out-think her, and he could outwit her if she wasn't careful. She was beginning to see that it was a compliment to her own intelligence that it had taken him as long as nine months to find her, not a compliment to his that he found her in only that amount of time.

She slid her long nightshirt over her slim shoulders and frowned ferociously into the slightly distorted mirror on the wall. Well, all that meant was that she was going to have to think harder, dig way down and really use her brains for the first time in a long time. The only reason why he had found her in the first place was because she had underestimated him and relaxed her guard. She had slipped up.

And she wasn't going to slip up again.

The bathroom door opened slowly, and she stuck her head around it hesitantly. There he was, reclining on the floor with his bare arms flexed back and hands linked behind his dark head. He was resting on one of the huge throw pillows that she used on her bed in the daytime, and her bedcovers were pulled down for her. The late news was on the television, but he was watching her instead, unwaveringly. A fresh wave of nervousness hit her in the region of her stomach and it showed. Her big blue eyes were nearly black, they were dilated so, and her thin face was very pale. She came out of the bathroom slowly, looking as if she might bolt at the first sudden movement.

Mike Carridine said calmly, running his unfathomable gaze down her slim body, 'I was beginning to get worried for a minute. I don't trust you in that bathroom for any length of time and I would hate to have to chase you in my pyjamas.'

Dee had to smile at that, reluctantly, and felt comfortable enough to walk closer. The room was so small that he had to lay down his blankets by necessity right beside her bed, and she climbed on her bed from the bottom end to avoid stepping over him. Then she settled gingerly under the covers, eyeing him with that wary, distrustful gaze.

His face softened a little, and the change in his expression from that was so noticeable that she had to stare. Those features were really hard, with a firm, uncompromising jaw and harsh cheekbones and browbone, and she'd only seen him with a determined look in those bright green eyes. That gentler expression made him look younger, and she found herself revising her impression of his age. He would be in his late twenties, perhaps, or thirty. 'You don't have anything to feel nervous about, child,' he said quietly. 'I won't hurt you.'

Her eyes widened at that, and she felt supremely startled. She was touched by what he had said, but then her facial expression sharpened and she snapped, 'I don't believe that, and I don't trust you. You're hurting me now, damn you, and there's nothing I can do about it!'

His eyes changed and they stared at each other for a minute before Dee deliberately rolled over and pulled her covers to her neck. There was a moment or two of tense silence and then something rustled. She stiffened, but all that happened was that the light was abruptly doused and they were plunged into darkness. The last thing said between them was when Mike said implacably, 'We leave in the morning, early.' And the words fell on her heart like a heavy stone.

Dee didn't sleep well at all, what with nervousness cramping in her stomach and apprehension holding her in its grip. She could hear Mike's quiet breathing, even and soft in the darkness, and the sound was strangely intimate and soothing. Even so, she had the impression of a coiled, dangerous animal crouching at her feet and she dared not move for fear she might wake the beast.

When the first golden rays began to dispel the predawn's greyness, she quietly crept out of her covers and went to her tiny kitchen to start the coffee. When she turned around and glanced at Mike, she found him watching her calmly, alertly, though he still looked relaxed. He also looked rested, which was more than she could say for herself. She put a selfconscious hand to her rumpled hair, blinking sleepily.

'I must look like a mess,' she mumbled, sliding her eyes away from his. In actuality she looked like a sleepy rumpled kitten, with those clear blue eyes peering out from under the yellow gold of her curling hair. The nightshirt was too large and merely served to emphasise the slight delicate lines of her bone structure, and drew attention to her legs.

'Mm,' was his only comment, but when Dee glanced up and caught his gaze, she saw appreciation flicker in them as he swept her over with an encompassing look. That made her more selfconscious than before, and she became aware of how much bare leg she was exposing. In comparison to her tiny bikini, it wasn't much, but the context of it was what had her blushing furiously. A quick second glance at him found him looking slightly amused, and this only served to make her redden even more. 'Who gets first dibs on the bathroom?'

She seized on that gratefully. 'I'll get in first, so that I can be packing while you're in.' And then, with a sudden forlorn look around, she added miserably, 'What's going to happen to all my things?' But she ducked her head without waiting for a reply, then turned to bring down a coffee mug from the cupboard, pouring some of the fresh hot liquid into it and handing it carefully to him, heart rattling madly away and mouth dry. She kept a stern hold on her expression, though, and her face was calm. Mike took it with a murmured thanks, and then glanced at her other empty hand curiously.

'You're not having any?' He sipped at the cup and winced at its heat.

'No,' she replied offhandedly, 'I want to take a shower first so that my hair can dry. Leave the burner on and I'll have some when I get out.'

He nodded, and she quickly escaped into the minuscule privacy of the bathroom, shutting the door and leaning against it, sagging. Then, shooting into frantic action, she jumped into the shower and was out again before the water had a chance to heat up. Towelling her hair dry and combing it with a ruthless disregard for the painful tangles, she was out again in about seven minutes. The drug was powerful and it would start to hit him soon. She found him partially dressed, with a pair of faded jeans on and a dark blue shirt, unbuttoned. He was sitting at the table and holding his head in one hand, and Dee felt a surge of guilt at what she had done. She advanced cautiously. 'How are you feeling? Are you getting disorientated?'

His head came up and he looked at her angrily. 'You drugged me, didn't you?' The words were angry, yet slurred, and she winced.

She didn't bother to lie. 'Yes, I did. I'm sorry, but I had to.'

She came over and put a hand on his arm, feeling the muscle bunch at her touch, so that she stepped back nervously. Would he get violent? He tried to stand and started to fall, and she ran to his side quickly, throwing her arms around his waist for support. She helped him to her bed and let him fall on it, stepping back pantingly. He was heavier than he looked. Then she sat on the edge of the bed and looked down at his face. It was strange, looking at him like this. He seemed so helpless, for all his smooth, latent muscled strength. He focussed his eyes with difficulty on her face, one hand coming up to cup her cheek, only to fall lifelessly on to the bed again.

Impulsively Dee reached out and smoothed hair away from his brow, and it was silky to the touch. 'How long do I have?' he muttered, fighting to keep his eyes open.

'Only a minute or so. They're strong sleeping pills,' she answered softly. Strange, to feel regret. 'You should be well rested by the time you wake up, in about five or six hours. I hope they don't give you a headache, like they did me.'

Mike sighed, resignedly, and incredibly his lips quirked into a fleeting smile. 'You little brat, why'd you go and do a thing like this for?'

'I'll run until I die,' she said quietly. 'No amount of coercion will change that. I will not be forced into something against my will. I tell you, I will not go back.'

'I'm going to come after you, you know that,' he whispered, closing his eyes and opening them again to stare at her. Dee was amazed that the sleeping pills would take so long to affect him. He should have been out cold long ago.

'Stubborn man!' she muttered, running her gaze over his face. He was a very handsome man, and she suddenly realised that she was resting one hand lightly against his bare chest.

He muttered mockingly, 'Stubborn child,' and his eyes fluttered shut for the last time.

Dee watched him sleeping as peacefully as a baby,

and she smiled a strange smile that she couldn't explain even to herself. 'Never underestimate your opponent, Mike Carridine. I'm no child.' And she touched his motionless lips with her own.

Even though she knew she had time, she raced around like a mad thing, stuffing essentials into her knapsack and cleaning out the coffee-maker. Then she thoughtfully prepared Mike a nice salad for lunch and tucked him under the covers so that he would be comfortable. She didn't know what appalled her the most: the fact that she had drugged him, or that she had actually kissed him, even if he was unconscious of that. She didn't know what crazy impulse had prompted her. After stuffing her handbag into her knapsack, she wrote out a hasty note, giggling a little nervously at its smart message: Take your time. There's lunch in the refrigerator. The rent's paid until the end of the month. Dee.

When she was ready to go, she stood for one last time and stared down into his face. The covers were pulled to his chest, but even so she could see a good expanse of brown skin. His head was turned to one side, and he was breathing deeply, evenly, peacefully. She had the suspicion that he wouldn't be so peaceful when he woke up, and she suddenly felt a chill of apprehension when she thought of what he might do if he actually caught up with her again. But she shrugged that away, and bent to press her soft lips against his warm forehead. Then she quietly shut and locked the door behind her as she left.

The lock on the door was an old one, the kind that you needed a key to unlock from either side. As she raced down the stairs, Dee wondered gleefully if he knew how to pick locks. If not, then he was going to have a hell of a time getting that door open, short of bursting through it. Once outside, she scampered nimbly over to his car and let out the air in all the tyres, leaving him a nicely detailed map, hastily drawn, showing him the route to the nearest gas station. She tucked that under a windshield wiper. Those delays might give her as much as an hour more, which was a nice chunk of time.

After all that, she turned and loped on down the street. When she came to the major four-lane highway that ran roughly north and south/southwest, she began to stick out her thumb. A few cars passed her by and a third began to slow, but she didn't like the look of the man in the driver's seat, so she ducked her head and ran left for a block or so. He would have to turn around and get in the other lane to come back after her, and a quick glance back showed that he hadn't bothered. Then a large truck was barrelling her way, and she stuck out her thumb in an effort to get the trucker's attention. At first she thought he was going to whizz on by, but then she heard a screeching of brakes and saw it lurch to a stop several yards ahead. Sending up a hopeful prayer, she ran back and just reached the cab of the truck when the passenger door was thrust open and a grizzled head popped out to shout at her cheerfully, 'Hey, little punkin, need a ride?'

'Oh, please!' she shouted back, over the powerful engine's roar. She was unaware of just how frightened she looked, with her blue eyes almost black and her cheeks flushed red from running. 'I'm in a bit of a hurry!'

'Well, sweet thing, climb on up and have a seat!' he roared, backing up so that she could haul herself in. She did so tremblingly, secretly amazed at how badly she was shaking. After all, what was there to be worried about? Everything was going her way so far that day. The trucker yelled cheerfully, 'I'm going way down south, and you're welcome for as long as you care to ride!'

Plopping down breathlessly on the wide seat, Dee

took stock of her surroundings and her new friend, and found that she liked both very much. The cab was neatly kept and well dusted, which spoke well for the driver's habits. The driver himself was around his fifties, with a powerful barrel chest and huge biceps. His face was clean-shaven and his faded blue eyes twinkled in a network of wrinkles from years of long-distance squinting. Dee was observant and quick in her character assessment, and when she saw the gold wedding band on his left hand, she breathed a sigh of relief. He seemed nice enough.

The truck was lurching forward with a roar, and the driver told her conversationally, 'My name's Chuck, Chuck Greenway, what's yours, punkin?'

'Deirdre,' she said loudly, having to speak over the truck's roar. 'But my friends call me Dee.' They hit a hole in the road and she bounced totally off her seat, making Chuck laugh heartily.

'Why, you ain't any bigger than my little grand-daughter, punkin!' he shouted gustily. 'What's a sweet thing like you doin' hitch-hiking around? Don't you know that's a good way to get hurt?'

'I'm running away!' she yelled blithely. 'My boy-friend's gotten a little rough with me lately, and I don't like being hit about! I'm going to try and get home to my grandparents, in Missouri.' It was as good a story as any, she shrugged. Maybe she could make Mike Carridine out as being the cruel boy-friend. It was a satisfying contemplation.

'That's bad, that's real bad! Why, I'd guess one good puff of wind would knock you down, sweet thing, let alone a good slap in the face!' said Chuck with a ready sympathy, shaking his grey head soberly. 'You reckon he's gonna come after you?'

'Probably,' she sighed. If Mike Carridine had trailed her for nine months, he wasn't about to stop now, like he'd said. Dee felt a wave of pure frustration quiver through her. In all the country, in the entire wide world, she couldn't shake one stubborn man off her trail. This was getting to be annoying.

'Well, punkin, you just let me know if you see him comin' and I'll take care of him for ya,' he told her comfortingly. 'A tiny little thing like you needs protection in this world, that's what. Protection in this world. What was your name? Deborah?'

'Dee!' she shouted, chuckling a little. It had been a risk, hitch-hiking like she had, but all the truck drivers she had met had been kindly, gruff men, and it had apparently been a risk well worth taking. By the end of the first hour, she and Chuck were fast friends, and by the end of the second, Dee knew the name of everyone in Chuck's rather extensive family. She listened with fascination as he conducted cheerful conversations on the CB radio, using jargon she only half comprehended.

'Hey, good buddy, I got me a pretty little yellow canary bird running away from a big bad cat, come back,' Chuck spoke into the receiver and, totally mystified, Dee listened for the reply.

'What's your big bad cat look like, little canary?' one of the truckers asked, and Chuck raised an eyebrow at Dee.

'Oh!' she fumbled, as realisation hit that she was the topic of the conversation. 'I—I don't know. You mean my boy-friend's car? It's a dark green, I don't know the make.'

Chuck gave her a look that plainly expressed that he hadn't expected any more from a woman, no matter how delightful she was, and Dee was hard put to it to keep from laughing as he went back to his conversation. Soon all of the truckers in northern Ohio knew about her and that she was running away from her boy-friend, the Big Bad Cat. She squirmed a little at the freedom with which they all cheerfully discussed her problem, and devoutly hoped that Carridine didn't have a CB in his car. If so, he would know her approximate direction and mode of travel before the day was out. She wished she had known what Chuck was about to say before he'd actually done it, but the damage was done now. There was no use moaning about it.

After a while, she began to get drowsy and she curled up in the seat, putting her tousled fair head on her knapsack and relaxing. She was more depressed than she had first realised. She would have to find a way to go back for some of her things. She slept.

'Hey, wake up, punkin! Wake up! Boy, you sure did sleep a lot!' Chuck shouted at her, shaking her with one hand on her slim shoulder. Dee sat up groggily and knuckled her eyes before staring out. The daylight was beginning to fade and evening was setting in. Everything looked unfamiliar. 'You gettin' hungry?'

She considered that. She hadn't eaten anything since the day before. 'Yes, I am. Where are we, Chuck?' The highway looked like a dark blue-grey ribbon in the fading light, and bright spots of yellow, red and blue from lit signs showed brilliantly as gas stations, restaurants and motels turned on their night signs. The surrounding countryside was fading from a dark green to a total black. 'Good God! Did I sleep the entire day away?'

'Just about! You fell asleep right around eleven, and it's gettin' pretty late right now! I stopped some time ago, but you were so dead you never noticed, and I didn't have the heart to wake ya! We're some distance just north of Cinncinatti. I got me a favourite truck stop of mine an' the boys, comin' up in a few miles. Called up on the CB and there's gonna be some friends of mine there, if you're willin' to eat then.'

'Sounds good. I'm ravenous!' Dee told him enthusiastically. He grinned and nodded, patting his own stomach in agreement with her. Dee rummaged around and brought her hairbrush out to straighten some of her tangles while she looked out of the window. She felt very strange, sitting up so high in the cab of the huge truck. Everything seemed so different.

After a little while, Chuck signalled and pulled off on to an exit ramp that swirled in a great spiral down, sending them back to the array of brightly lit buildings easily seen from the highway. He then expertly parked the monstrous vehicle and turned off the engine. Both of them jumped to the ground, Dee finding her legs stiff from staying in one position for so long. It was greatly refreshing to be able to walk about, and she sighed with pleasure as a cool wind blew gently against her cheek.

'This way, punkin,' Chuck told her, gesturing to a rather dirty white, one-story building with a neon sign splashed on the roof. 'I don't know about you, but I need to use the little boys' room.'

Dee giggled at him and fell into step beside him, with her knapsack slung over one shoulder. He held open the door for her and followed behind, pointing out the way to the public restrooms. After she had used the facilities and had straightened her appearance, she went back out to be eyed curiously by several unknown men. Just as she was beginning to feel nervous about it, Chuck barrelled into the dining area and swept past her to start pumping hands all around. He then introduced her to everyone, including with their real names each one's CB pseudonym, and she started to relax when she recognised a few of the men she had talked to that afternoon.

They were all a cheerful, easygoing bunch, and Dee was treated like a fragile queen, which she loved, but she was under no illusions about some of the men. If she hadn't been under Chuck's protection and with several of his friends, she wouldn't have liked to bet on her chances with some of the rougher-looking types. As it was, she was sandwiched in firmly between Chuck and one of his buddies, a younger fellow every bit as rough and gruff as Chuck, and if anyone happened to leer too long in her general direction, he was treated with a wide-eyed, warning stare from either of the two men.

Supper was hot and hearty and conversation sharply decreased while everyone tucked into their supper. Dee had to smile several times during the course of her meal. Her presence really overthrew the natural flow of conversation for the men, she could see. Many times someone would start to make a ribald joke or a crude comment, and he would fall silent in the middle of the statement. Already her vocabulary picked up at the restaurant had been increased by several words and phrases, some of which she made a mental note to look up in the dictionary or ask someone about, if the dictionary happened to be too clean.

Chuck insisted on buying her a dish of ice cream when everyone had coffee, so she tucked into that with enjoyment. She was just licking her spoon and contemplating her steaming cup of hot brew with pleasure when the glass door at the entrance swung open and a dark man walked quietly in. Dee glanced up casually, caught sight of the man and promptly dropped her spoon in consternation, though with no great surprise.

Mike's silent green gaze swept over the dining area and came to rest on her. She sighed as he gave her a short, perfunctory nod and immediately headed her way. Chuck glanced at her. 'Hey, you gotta drink up your coffee before it gets too cold.' Really, she thought with amused exasperation, he's worse than a fussy old grandmother! He saw the expression on her face and looked in the direction her eyes were trained. 'Is that the boy-friend, punkin?'

'I guess you could call him that,' she said tartly. He was sure sticking as close as a lover! If only that were the problem.

Mike was silently passing occupied booths and Dee thought his very quietness was more menacing than all of the bluster in the world. His face looked hard and set, and his eyes glittered, sending off sparks of something volatile that Dee thought would be better left unexpressed.

Sliding casually out of the booth, Chuck came out before Mike to block his way and was immediately joined by Fred. That husky fellow, for all his earlier good humour, was beginning to look pugnacious. Dee began to feel alarmed.

'Hey there,' Chuck said heartily. 'How ya doin', old buddy? What do you need? If you're wantin' a meal to eat, there's plenty of tables in the other direction.'

Mike looked beyond him to Dee, his expression unreadable as he stared into her suddenly huge, apprehensive eyes. 'I want to talk to the young lady over there,' he said quietly, in his pleasant low voice. He hadn't even acknowledged the threat in Chuck's overly hearty speech by so much as a blink of the eyes. All his attention was focussed on Dee's face. He was as tenacious as a bulldog. Dee smelled the danger hanging like sulphur in the air and she silently swore, Damn him! Why didn't he just leave? Why was he taking such a risk?

'We-ell,' Chuck drawled slowly, 'I don't think the little lady wants to talk to you. She's busy eatin' her supper, and you just might give her indigestion. We wouldn't want to do that, now, would we? She's such a sweet little ol' thing.' He took a step further and Fred touched shoulders with him as they blocked Dee's view of Mike. The potential for physical violence was there, like explosive dynamite, and without being aware of her intention, Dee was standing in the booth to perch herself so that she could see Mike's face. His green, implacable eyes sought hers. A nervous waitress shifted from one foot to the other, behind a counter.

Dee tried to signal frantically to Mike with her eyes, jerking her head to the door in an attempt to get him to leave. He watched her silently, from under level brows, taking in the anxiety so obvious in her blue eyes, and then he deliberately walked forward.

Both Fred and Chuck moved simultaneously, and one of Fred's hands came out to knock at Mike's shoulder to push him roughly back. But Mike wasn't there, as he pivoted neatly on one foot, quick as a snake, to avoid the shove and parry with one of his own. In that brief moment, Dee realised as she watched Mike's controlled speed that he could have taken care of both Fred and Chuck for all their bulk and strength, and won, if it hadn't been for the fellows that came up behind him to grasp his arms and twist them tightly behind his back. Mike's eyes came back to Dee's as his back arched agonisingly and his head jerked up, nostrils flaring, and Chuck's arm was swinging back for a blow when she galvanised into action.

She launched from the back of the booth where she had been perched and moved so swiftly that she had a hold of Chuck's clenched fist and was dragging on it with all her strength as she screamed, 'Don't hurt him!'

Chuck's eyes widened at this and he turned immediately into the gentle gruff man that she knew, putting his arm around her shaking shoulders and saying, 'Why, little punkin, it's gonna be all right. We're just gonna make sure that he don't give you any more scares, that's all.'

Dee was tired of being treated like a precious imbecile, and she snapped irritably, 'And what do you think you're doing to me, right now? Do you think this isn't scaring me half to death? And who gives you the right, anyway?' Neither of them saw the gleam of satisfaction in Mike's eyes, quickly veiled. 'I can take care of myself! I know how to hit, too, if I need to, you know!'

There were chuckles all around at this and somebody muttered, 'The little canary's turned out to be a tigress after all!' Chuck grinned amicably and stepped back, and the binding hands on Mike's twisted arms fell away. He straightened slowly, intent on the two in front of him.

'Why, punkin, you just go right ahead,' Chuck told her. 'But just the same, I think you'd better have your conversation in here, so's we can keep an eye on you.'

Dee nodded shortly, her anger fading. 'Thanks, Chuck,' she said, laying a hand lightly on his arm, and it was covered and squeezed gently.

'Any time, punkin. I reckon you two need to work things out between you anyways.' He sat down and everyone generally relaxed, but she was extremely aware of his sharp eye on them while he sipped his coffee. Mike saw, too.

Dee stared up at Mike, taking in his generally unruffled demeanour, and retorted, 'You really are a clever one, Mike Carridine! Yes, I'll have a cup of coffee with you! But don't you start taking it for granted that I'm going to go anywhere with you!' This last was said with a quick shake of a finger under Mike's nose, and she heard sniggers around her.

'Come on,' he said, taking her gently by the arm and leading her away to a corner table, out of earshot from everyone else. She slid into a chair while he ordered coffee for the two of them, morosely studying the man across from her from under blonde, lowered brows.

'How did you know I would react the way I did?' she asked abruptly. 'It was a good guess.'

He shrugged gracefully, hunching one shoulder and leaning his chin in one hand. 'I've had to study your character all this time, to try to figure out what you would have done in different situations that had confronted you. I've talked to people from the University, and I think I have a generally good impression of everyone's view of you. One thing you aren't is bloodthirsty.'

'Don't push it too far,' she warned him darkly, and had to grin reluctantly when he laughed. Her blue eyes became contemplative, mocking. 'So you think you know me that well, hmm?'

'Quite the contrary,' she was told immediately. 'I only know other people's impression of you. I'm only now beginning to form some impressions of my own, having met you. The only thing I can say with certainty about you is that I've underestimated you time and time again. In fact,' and his gaze flickered over to where Chuck was sitting, 'I'm beginning to think that the majority of people underestimate your potential, Dee.'

She had to feel flattered in spite of herself, but was quick to change the subject since she considered the conversation rather irrelevant. 'You have, I take it, a CB radio?'

His gaze became mocking and one corner of his mouth quirked. 'But of course. I'm the big bad cat, am I?'

She snorted with derision. 'He was on the radio and blabbing to everyone in the CB world before I could stop him. By the time I could sift through the jargon and understand what he was talking about, the damage was done.' She put up her hands and rubbed at her eyes tiredly. In spite of the sleep she had snatched in the truck, she felt tired from the upsets of the last two days. 'How did you feel when you woke up?'

'I had a headache,' he replied sourly, his expression wry. Dee noted absently that his nose looked as if it had been broken in a fight. He really was very handsome, she thought, and was mildly surprised that, aside from some exasperation, he didn't appear to be angry. 'And when I found the door locked on me and my tyres completely, utterly flat, I wanted to turn you over my knee and make your backside black and blue. But I've calmed down a bit.' He paused and then admitted ruefully, 'I guess I had it coming to me, though, for ever letting my guard slip. So, now what?'

'What, what?' she asked, and laughed. 'I'm so tired!'

'I know,' he said, and it was gentle, making her look at him in surprise. He was regarding her seriously. 'What are you going to do, Dee? Are you going to come with me, or are you going to go with Chuck and his friends?'

'And if I go with Chuck?' she asked, sending a lightning-swift, dagger-bright glance his way. He looked about as movable or as shakeable as a brick wall.

'Then I follow.' There was no hesitation.

Her brows shot up. 'It's a good way to get hurt, you know.'

'I know. I'll risk it.' He didn't, she thought angrily, look worried.

Dee muttered tiredly, feeling dispirited, 'Why don't you go away?'

He responded promptly, 'Why don't you go home? There's a lot of people worried about you.'

'Oh, hell!' she burst out, supremely angry, and his eyes flared before becoming shadowed. 'Don't spit that nonsense to me!' She leaned forward. 'Are you trying to make me feel guilty in case you get hurt? I'm not responsible for your actions. If you follow me, then it's on your head!'

'I wouldn't presume to make you feel responsible for my actions,' he said quietly. 'I'm merely hoping to influence your decision. It worked just now. You couldn't bear to see me get my face bashed in, could you?'

She buried her face in her hands and tried to think. In spite of her brave and callous-sounding words, she knew she would feel guilty if he got hurt because of her. He was just doing his job.

In favour of her leaving with him was the fact that

she could still slip away, because there was a lot of ground to cover between here and home. And when she had appeased her own conscience by knowing he would not be hurt directly as a result from following her, then she would try again. Her shoulders slumped even more, dejectedly, since she knew he was watching her. 'All right,' she whispered softly, 'I'll go with you.'

CHAPTER FOUR

AFTER goodbyes had been said to Dee's trucker friends, Mike ushered her out of the restaurant and into his car. She'd remembered correctly—it was a dark green, sleek-modelled sedan car, built for comfort and durability. She slid into the passenger side willingly enough and curled her legs underneath her, resting her head against the back of the seat. Mike soon got in on the driver's side, and with one frowning glance at her tired face and exhausted demeanour, he leaned forward to switch on the ignition. Then he pulled into the curve that led on to the highway and they were heading south. Dee dozed in her seat while he drove into the night.

He didn't stay on the highway for long, however, and the change in the car's rhythmic purr woke her up. She sat straight up and looked dazedly around her, pushing the tangled blonde hair off her forehead. Mike pulled into another travelling oasis and parked smoothly in front of a motel. He said quietly, 'You look about ready to call it a night.'

She merely nodded. He got out and came around to her side to open the door for her. As she hesitated, he told her, a thread of amusement running through his low voice, 'Tired though you may be, I don't think I'd trust you as far as I could throw you. If you wouldn't mind, I'd like your company while I register for a room.'

She grimaced and heard him laugh, and who could blame him? she thought. I wouldn't trust myself either. Sliding out of her seat, she stuck her hands into her front pockets and joined him as he went into the motel's office. Behind the counter was a scruffy little man with a drooping moustache. He was reading a dog-eared Western novel and looked up uninterestedly as they entered. Mike went forward and requested a double room for one night, and Dee flushed as the greasy little man's eyes slid over her with an oily, insinuating look. But one glance at the set face of the man in front of him quelled any remark he might have made, and he sullenly asked for the payment for the room. Mike gave him some bills, received a key, and then turned away from the counter, his dark face holding a fleeting look of disgust.

She had been looking at him thoughtfully, her large blue eyes understanding, and for one moment they were both in perfect accord as his eyes met hers. He smiled then, wryly, and put a casual hand on her shoulder as they walked out of the office. 'Sorry about that.'

She was concentrating on her own mixed-up emotions. 'Why?'

'I wish you hadn't had to see that greasy little bug back there,' he said a little tightly. 'I didn't mean for that to happen.'

'Oh!' she replied, a little fluster and then amused. 'You mean that guy thinking we were having a one-night stand?'

He gave her one look, a swift piercing glance. 'That's exactly what I mean. I won't let you have a room of your own, you know.'

'But of course not!' she exclaimed, surprised. 'I would have been astonished if you had. I certainly didn't expect to.' She heard a low, masculine laugh, and her brows shot up as she realised that he was shaking his head and chuckling.

'You amaze me at every turn!' he told her. 'I half expected a tantrum or perhaps a show of hostility when I caught up with you this time, but you calmly tell me you hadn't expected anything else. And now this . . . the things you manage to take into stride! You're something special, Dee.'

'I like to think so,' she murmured, taken aback at his words of praise. She then noticed the suitcase he hauled out of the trunk, along with his own. 'Oh, marvellous! You brought some of my clothes! Thank you very much.'

'You're welcome,' he replied, still laughing at her. They strolled along the shadowy sidewalk, looking at room numbers on each door, and when they came to their room, he stopped, put down the suitcases, and unlocked the door. She went on ahead of him and turned on a few light switches while he deposited their suitcases on the two beds before locking and bolting the door.

She sank on to one bed and asked him interestedly, 'So you really understood why I drugged you?'

Mike hesitated and then admitted slowly, 'I'm beginning to see your perspective a bit, yes.'

'That's a handsome thing to admit—and by the way, I do feel awful about that, really. I'd never done anything like that in my life. And I think you're taking it amazingly well.'

A strange, slight smile split the hard quality of his features. She felt something hit her in the region of her stomach and she stared, obviously. The gleam of his white teeth showed against a naturally dark complexion tanned to an even darker brown. He dragged a chair around and relaxed into it, and she was struck anew at his long length when he stretched out his legs, much like the earlier afternoon.

'Perhaps it's because I sympathise with you more than I should,' he murmured, and she felt so jolted by that admission, she didn't know what to say. There was a strange look invading his eyes, making them cloudy. 'You feel threatened; it's understandable. Besides, as I said before, if I'm that easy to dupe, then I deserve to be drugged. It'll teach me a lesson.'

'Never to trust me again, I'll bet!' laughed Dee, her

eyes crinkling at him. She saw his widen briefly before his lids came down to hide them. 'You know, I have to say I really admire your work. You've done an excellent job hunting me down. It's nothing short of incredible how you've managed to unravel my tangled trail.'

'I thank you,' he replied, with a jaunty inclination of his head. 'And I should return the compliment by saying that I can't remember when I've felt so challenged. Your brain must be very twisted to come up with some of the stunts you pulled. That was very clever, hiding away in the attic to wait for the uproar of your disappearance to go elsewhere. The one place in the world where no one thought to look. Well done, indeed!'

She felt a flicker of uneasiness lick at her mind again. This man was so frighteningly, formidably alert—only one person in a thousand could have guessed her ruse from that night. And she was pitting her wits against him. She felt a sudden keen regret that fate had placed her in opposition with him. She liked and admired him. 'How did you know I'd camped in the attic?'

'Merely chance. After a few days of checking around the airports and bus depots, I returned to the scene of departure and went over your room inch by inch,' he explained, putting a lean fingered hand up to rub at the back of his neck. 'When I idly pushed on the loose panel of wood that lay across the hole, I realised I'd hit pay dirt. That was when I finally began to realise what kind of intelligence I was up against. Fresh breadcrumbs and a half used gallon jug of water gave you away, I'm afraid.'

'I'd forgotten about that?' Dee shook her head at her own forgetfulness. 'Well, it served its purpose at the time.'

'Served its purpose quite well, I should think,' retorted Mike, standing to go over to the phone and picking up the phone book lying beside it. 'I'd been meaning to ask you—were you the smart aleck who called the press and told them you were missing?'

She gurgled with laughter. 'Yes, I am. It was the only way I could think of to handicap your movements. Did it work?'

'Infuriatingly. I swore several times that when I caught up with you, I'd wring your pretty little neck! Would you like some pizza?' he asked, running a neatly manicured finger down one side of the page slowly.

'N-not really,' she murmured, feeling very full from her supper. 'I had quite a bit to eat just a little while ago. I might manage a piece or two. Are you hungry?'

'Starving,' he told her, 'famished, and otherwise ravenous. I haven't eaten since early this afternoon, and for some inexplicable reason seemed to lose my appetite at the truck stop.' His finger stopped for a moment.

Dee felt just terrible as a pang of guilt shot through her. For the first time she realised just how much she had upset this man's life, dragging him all over the country and upsetting his schedule. Her jaw and eyes hardened at that thought, and she got angry at herself for getting too sympathetic with someone who was perfectly able to take care of himself. He had taken the job. It wasn't her fault that he had galloped all over the place, looking for her. And he probably was well paid for it, too.

Mike glanced up just then and caught the hardened, bitter look on her tired face, and his own expression changed. Putting down the phone book, he crossed his arms in front of his wide chest and kicked one leg over the other. 'You've just remembered, haven't you?' he murmured. 'For a few hours you actually forgot that I'm the bad guy in this situation.'

And suddenly the veneer was stripped away and she was seeing again the purpose behind all the charm and pleasantness, and a feeling of anger and, strangely, loss welled up inside her. Being lonely when one is not alone is a frustrating emotion, and she experienced it as she stared across the room at the man who was against her at every turn. 'Well?' she asked, flippant and not caring that she was. 'Aren't you? Just along with all the others who never took the time to ask what would make me happy, instead of telling me? Pardon me, mister, but I don't think very highly of your methods!'

A brow cocked at that. He was angry. 'And you're the original "poor little rich girl", is that it? The usual outcry of the teenager—nobody understands me! Do you have any idea of the amount of worry and care and trouble that you've brought to so many people? Do you even care?'

It had been quite some time since she had thought of herself as an adolescent, and the suspicion that he thought of her as such hurt unbearably. She felt a wave of fury so deeply intense that she wasn't sure she could control it, and she stood, her eyes blazing brilliantly in her suddenly white face. They looked like jewels, liquid and sparkling, and the man across the room watched her intently. For a moment she wasn't sure if she was going to walk up to him and slap his face hard or walk out of the room, and the struggle for control seemed to take forever, though in actuality it was only a few moments. She just looked at him, turned on her heel, and headed for the bathroom.

Suddenly he was there, grabbing her shoulders and forcing her to turn around, and this was heaping insult upon injury. Her eyes spat hatred at him; how could she have considered him someone she could like and respect? 'Running away seemed to be a habit with you!' he gritted between his teeth. 'Perhaps it's because you don't want to grow up, is that it? You can't stand it when things don't go your own way, can you?'

She thought the top of her head would come off with the pressure of trying to keep her temper in control, and she said slowly, measuringly, bitingly, 'I am not, as you so eloquently put it, "running away" from what you have to say. I merely think it's unimportant and irrelevant to this topic of conversation.' She paused and drew in a deep breath, and it sounded ragged even to her own ears. 'I know more than you could just exactly the extent of worry I caused some people, and frankly it leaves me unimpressed. I suggest that you keep both your hands and your meaningless homilies to yourself until you know the full situation and know just what the hell you're talking about!' With her two hands stiffened, she swept his off her shoulders, then left the room with dignity.

Mike stood a long time, just staring after her, in the middle of the room after she had disappeared.

Dee sank down to the floor in the bathroom, her leg muscles quivering weakly from reaction. She was appalled to think of the two of them, apparently rational and calm-tempered people, just blowing up at each other like they had. Granted, the last few days had been a bit hectic, but that last tangle had not been at all what a hired private investigator and a found runaway would normally have had. It was more—personal than that. It shouldn't have been. They were in opposition with each other on an issue that should be the sole point of contention between them, and yet it was pushed to a level beyond that. He had actually been angry, deeply, emotionally upset at something just now, and she—well, she had felt somehow betrayed by his reaction to a situation that he should not be personally involved in. And the question that she asked herself was, why?

It was all too tangled for her to fathom. Life, nine months ago, had been much more black and white, the good guys and the bad, the prison and the escape. And now she was tired and she was lonely, and she only wanted to live her life in peace. She never wanted to hear Mike Carridine's name again. And this thought made her very upset, because she knew it to be a lie.

After a time she stirred and reached out a lethargic hand to turn on the water taps for a bath. Steaming hot water gushed out and she stripped eagerly. She was aching, and a soak in the tub would do her good. She sank into the painfully warm wetness with many sighs and upstarts from the heat. Then, as her body adjusted to the temperature, she leaned back and closed her eyes. Some time later, she sudsed busily and rinsed herself, and as she rose out of the tub, she realised that she didn't have any clean clothes with her. She hated to get dressed just to get her nightshirt, just to come back and change again, so she called out, 'Mike? Mike?'

Footsteps sounded just outside the door and his voice wafted through the barrier. 'What do you need?' His tone seemed much milder and she felt relieved.

'Could you dig in my suitcase—no, wait! My knapsack has it—could you bring me my nightshirt? I forgot to bring it in with me.'

'Just a moment.' Footsteps receded and a moment ticked by, then he was rapping at the door of the bathroom. 'I'll leave it by the door.'

Dee grabbed the towel and wrapped it tightly around her. 'Don't bother, I'm decent enough. Here——' And she opened the door to encounter his gaze with something like shock quivering through them both. He handed her the small bundle of material and she thanked him gravely. Something showed in his face, very briefly, as his eyes travelled down the length of her involuntarily, touching on the long slim legs, the finely shaped, glistening collarbones, the grace of her wet bare arms. Her eyes were an enormous, sapphire blue, and her expression was uncertain.

Then Mike was backing up and shutting the door, leaving her to wonder shakily what that look had been about.

She yanked her over-large shirt over her head and found as she shook out the garment that a filmy white flutter fell to the ground. It was a clean pair of panties, and she flushed at his thoughtfulness, feeling embarrassed.

In the other room, as she entered it, she found him lounging on the bed that he had claimed for his own, shoes off and one leg propped casually up with the other stretched full out. His gaze was fixed on the television screen directly opposite him and she realised that the late movie was on. He had an open cardboard box on a chair dragged over by the bed, and she saw that it was a pizza, with several pieces already gone. When her eyes went back to his face, she saw that he was intent, abstracted, his lean face sombre and his eyes withdrawn.

She excused herself politely as she walked in front of the television and refused, as politely, his offer of pizza. Soon she was cross-legged on her own bed, brushing out her hair thoughtfully, staring at the opposite wall.

An abrupt movement made her look up enquiringly to meet Mike's brooding gaze. 'I don't want to hear that motel door open,' he said pointedly, nodding to the outside door. Dee just stared at him blankly, saw his lips thin with exasperation, then he picked up his small toilet case to stalk into the bathroom.

Her gaze swept to the door and she briefly considered making a dash for it. But he was too alert for that, she knew, and he would be after her so fast it wouldn't be worth the effort. She was too tired, anyway.

However, she mused, slanting a glance to her jeans by the bed . . . She tore into them in record time, and was sliding under the covers with her legs well hidden by the time the bathroom door opened again. When Mike came out she was pulling the covers up to her chin and peering over the edge doubtfully at him.

His lips twisted, but whatever he was thinking he

didn't say, as he sat on the edge of his own bed with his
back to her. Off came his shirt, and she ran her eyes
over his beautiful back, already able to recognise that
neat taper down to a slim waist. His rib cage rippled
under sleek muscles and he stood, hands at his waist,
unfastening his slacks.

Dee turned her head away at this, not wanting to see
what happened next. Obviously he was not embarrassed
about someone seeing his naked body. He was, after all,
much older than she. He had probably disrobed for a
woman before. She suddenly had a burning curiosity,
wondering if he would sleep in the raw tonight, but she
didn't have the courage to turn around and look.

A tiny click plunged them both into darkness and she
turned at that to see a shadowy large figure move for
the other bed and climb in with a creaking of bed-
springs. Illogically, Dee felt frustrated at the cloaking
darkness that hid the sight of his body from her seeking
gaze, and that was a thought that brought her up short,
disconcerted.

Silence. She couldn't hear his breathing across the
room, and that was nerve-racking. She pinched herself,
bit her lip nervously until it bled, and thought of the
most exhilarating and exciting things she could imagine
in an effort to stay awake. Frustration gnawed away
inside of her because she wouldn't let herself toss and
turn to relieve the tension. It was hard to stay awake,
very hard, and time ticked away slowly—too slowly.
She waited and her lip bled sickeningly where she had
bit it, and she stared up at the blackness directly
overhead that was the ceiling. After an eternity she
reached very, very carefully over the edge of her bed
and picked up her slim gold watch. Bringing it close to
her eyes and turning it this way and that, she was finally
able to make out the time. Close to four o'clock. There
was absolutely no movement from the other bed, no
indication whether he was awake or not.

She would just have to chance it. If he was awake, well then, the only thing that could happen was that he would catch her, and that didn't bother her at all.

It did, really, but she wasn't going to let that stop her from trying. Her hands slid down to her sweater and her socks and shoes stacked neatly together, grasping that with one hand while the other groped for her handbag. A second of panic gripped her when she thought she might have left it over on the other side of the room, but then her hand encountered the smooth, cool leather strap and she picked it up silently. Then her legs slid to the side of the bed and she started to stand very carefully, slowly. The bed didn't even sigh.

She didn't want to risk making a noise in an attempt to slip into the rest of her clothes, and by now it was late enough so that everyone should be asleep and the parking lot deserted. She'd put everything on just outside the door.

Silent as a wraith, she glided over the floor to the door, and had to put down some of her things to feel delicately for the lock and bolt. Catching her fingers on something, she grasped the thing protruding out about shoulder-high and pushed very, very carefully, experimentally. The bolt slid open without a sound, and she then reached for the doorknob to turn the lock there. The darkness behind her was completely silent, and she wanted to call out to him to say goodbye, a strange, insane desire that had her nearly laughing out loud. Picking up the clothes that she had put down and shifting her handbag to one shoulder, she grasped the knob and hesitated briefly. There was nothing else for it but to open the door as quickly and as silently possible and to pray that the cold night air didn't wake him.

She turned the knob, pulled the door slightly open and slipped through to shut it immediately. She shivered convulsively as the night wind brushed her bare arms. Only vaguely did she take in the sound of

low voices close by, and she didn't even see the two
shadowy figures on the other side of the car parked
three spaces down. She slipped her things on to the
ground and swiftly tucked her nightshirt into her jeans,
pulling on her black sweater with shaking hands.

She didn't stay just outside the door to put on her
socks and shoes but instead inched delicately away,
shuddering as the cold cement under her feet turned
them into blocks of ice. Propping her bag on the hood
of Mike's car, she slipped on her shoes and socks—then
gagged from shock when a low masculine voice
sounded right by her ear. He had heard her! But then
she realised that the voice had come from behind the
car, not by the motel door, and this sent fear zigzagging
down her spine in an electric jolt.

'Hey, cute thing, where you goin', so late at night?'
the strange voice asked her, and she started to back
away, nearly screaming when she came up against
something solid. In fact, she thought about it and then
would have screamed anyway to wake Mike up and let
him know she was in trouble, but a rough hand
clamped down over her lips and a low voice
admonished her to be silent.

There was no choice about that, with that biting
hand gripping her so hard, but she wasn't going to
just stand there passively. The man gripping her
privately marvelled at how violent such a little thing
could be. She writhed and kicked and squirmed
grimly, determined to hurt as much as she possibly
could, but he was far stronger than she, and the
element of surprise had been to his favour. Then the
other man was cursing and grabbing her arms with a
bruising pressure, both of them forcing her away from
the building.

There was more low curses as some of her wild
blows hit home. The second man holding her arms
swore vulgarly as her kicking landed a vicious blow on

his shin, but he soon put an end to that by reaching down and wrapping both arms around her flailing legs. That left her hands free, and she suddenly reached back to scratch hard at the face of the man behind her. His head jerked back to avoid those wounding, dangerous claws, and his grip loosened enough on her mouth for her to be able to force her jaws open and fasten her teeth into the soft, fleshy part of his hand. She bit with every particle of strength in her, with the tenacity of a fighting wildcat, and briefly tasted something sour before a warm, salty spurt of blood filled her mouth. The man hissed in pain and rage, and he landed a heavy, stunning blow to the side of her head, making the world jerk sickeningly, but Dee didn't let go. She wanted to be sure she would have time enough for one lung-bursting, ear-splitting, peace-shattering scream, for the only sounds so far had been the men's low cursing and her own sobbing breaths. She almost made it; she would have made it, except that the other man taking in his accomplice's pain, loosened his hold on her legs and fastened his heavy hands on her neck.

The weight on her throat tightened cruelly, cutting off her air and making her see stars dance behind her closed eyelids. She kept her grip on the other man's hand, though, biting as deeply and as viciously as she could, but soon her lungs were bursting from lack of fresh air, and her head swam dizzily, her consciousness beginning to recede. Her mind was divided into two parts: the one part totally wrapped up in her desperate, physical struggle and pain, and the other part simply incredulous that this was really happening to her. As she slumped in her attacker's arms, so did her jaw relax her death clench on the one man's hand, and it was jerked away. She was barely conscious of it happening, for she was going under into a murky blackness, her hands pounding weakly on the man strangling her. The passage of time from the moment she had stepped out of the motel room to now had been perhaps three minutes, if that.

She began to die.

Mike was stronger than the man in front of him, and he had to his advantage the element of surprise, so the chopping blow that fell on the back of the man's neck caught him off guard and he slumped over, stunned. Then Mike was advancing on the man who had his hands on Dee's neck, his normally calm façade cracked into a ferocious snarl of rage as he took in her drooping slight figure, and then the man holding her was tossing her aside like a paper doll tossed to the wind. He turned to Mike and had just enough light to see blazing, searing, feral green eyes glint at him, and had just enough time to wonder if a man was attacking him or a wild beast. Then Mike launched a blow right out for his face, and he had no more time to think of anything but survival.

That awful blackness receded, and Dee was able to gulp frantically at the sweet, cold, life-sustaining air, retching slightly from the terrible pressure that had been on her neck. Both her hands were around her bruised and swollen throat, and she fought her way back to consciousness with grim determination. She wasn't to know that one of the men was already half-conscious on the ground, because her vision had not yet cleared. All she could think of was that there were two of them against only Mike. She didn't bother to analyse just how she knew that it was Mike. Some sixth sense told her, and he was fighting all by himself. And he was in danger. She turned, crouched on the pavement, one hand still at her aching throat, one hand on the ground for balance, and she saw two panting, plunging, heaving figures in front of her. One of them managed to get back far enough for a blow, and there was a grunt of pain from the one struck, a *whoof*! of expelled air. It went right to her heart, for she imagined that it was Mike, and she was so close to them both she could have reached out a hand to touch either of their legs.

A pale gleam of moonlight struck light blond hair on the man fighting closest to her, and she smiled a wicked smile as she realised that the man in front of her was not Mike. And it was never a good thing to turn one's back to Dee.

Both hands went down to the pavement, her crouching body drew into itself tightly, and then, with all of the speed and the force that she could impel into her right, powerful leg, she swung out and knocked out both of the man's legs right out from under him, felling him like a tree. Both of them cried out in pain, for he fell awkwardly, badly, heavily, and Dee bruised herself painfully from the force of her blow connecting with hard shin.

Mike's powerful body blurred with movement and the fallen attacker doubled up on himself, moaning. Then Dee cried out and pointed behind him where the first man was heaving himself to his feet. He didn't remain standing for long.

Mike stepped over the prone figure between himself and Dee, bending to the ground and picking her up as carefully and as tenderly as if she'd been made of fragile blown glass.

That gentleness, in comparison with his earlier deadly violence, completely shattered what was left of her composure. She crossed her arms tremblingly around his neck, bent at the middle, and started to cry painful, racking, hoarse sobs that tore through her body with the ferocity of a tropical storm. She was barely aware of Mike lifting her up and carrying her over the two sprawling figures. She sensed the passage from open night to the darkness of the inside building, and Mike laid her carefully down on one of the beds. He vanished briefly into blackness and in a few moments light was flooding throughout the room, making her close her eyes tightly.

Thus she didn't see the look of profound, intense shock that quivered over Mike's already white features as he looked at her. She was doubled up on the bed, arms crossed around her middle, instinctively protective, and her blonde hair was tangled and smeared with blood. One side of her face was already swollen from the blow she had sustained, and there were dark, ugly welts appearing on her slender neck. Her mouth and lower face were streaked with blood that had spurted when she had bitten her attacker. He stood stick, rigid still for a moment, like stone, and then he ran swiftly to the bathroom, emerging scant moments later with a cold wet hand towel. He knelt by the bed and touched her gently, making her start violently, and then he was wiping very carefully at her face, checking all the while for some deep cut or abrasion. The towel was regulation motel issue, basic white, and it was soon covered with bright red, making him swallow at the sight.

She sighed with pleasure at the cold wet cloth passing over her heated, hurting face and neck. She closed her eyes and turned her face to his gentle fingers. She hurt so, all over her body. It was very strange, because she didn't remember being knocked in some of the places where she ached.

'Dee,' he said lowly, and the sound of it was urgent. She looked at him questioningly. 'Where are you bleeding?'

'What?' she asked him blankly. It must be shock, she decided, this deadened feeling. She had meant to ask Mike what he had meant, but nothing had come from her mouth. Her tongue came out to moisten her bruised lips and then she tried again. This time it was she who was profoundly shocked at the hoarse croak that issued from her vocal cords. It hurt, and she put up a hand to massage her neck, fleetingly surprised at the sensation of violent tremors from her unsteady fingers brushing her neck. She tried again, 'What do you mean? I'm not bleeding.'

'Sweetheart,' he said gently, holding the bloodied towel in front of her face, 'look at this. This is blood, from you. Can you tell me if you hurt anywhere?' One hand came up under her hair and probed her skull carefully.

'It's not mine,' she whispered painfully. 'I bit one of those fellows and wouldn't let go. That's why the other one was choking me. It tasted horrible!' She shuddered at the memory.

The blank look on his face would have been ludicrous to see, had she noticed, but she was busy looking at the dark purple mark on his jawline and the harsh abrasion on his neck. She took the towel from him and wiped at the cut. He didn't even appear to notice. His eyes were trained on her face, then he rose abruptly to stride over to the door and open it to look out. A wry look passed over his face, and he disappeared a moment to come back with her purse, shutting the door and locking it.

'They're gone, of course. We certainly gave them enough time for it! I should have called the police right away, but the sight of the blood on your face—distracted me a bit.'

'Well!' she croaked emphatically. 'I'm glad I distracted you, then. The last thing we need right now is the police and all those questions ... you aren't still thinking of calling them, are you?' Her throat hurt so, and she longed for a drink.

He ran a keen look down her swiftly. 'I can't really see the point, now. And you're right, the last thing we need is uncomfortable questions.' He came over to sit down beside her and the bed creaked under his weight. 'Let me see your poor face ... you're going to have quite a collection of bruises, I'm sorry to say. How's your throat?'

His kindness and his gentle touch just about destroyed her newly won, precarious control again, and her eyes shimmered with unshed tears. 'It's okay,' she whispered brokenly. 'I'm lying, it hurts like hell. I need a drink of water.' He rose immediately and unwrapped a clean glass from the tray provided by the motel, fetching fresh water for her. Without waiting for her to sit up, he slid a strong arm underneath her shoulders to ease her up into a position comfortable for drinking, and she grasped the glass greedily. When it was drained, she relaxed back on his arm, grateful for its support. And suddenly she broke up completely, her face crumpling and hands fluttering tentatively out to him as she sobbed, 'I'm sorry! I'm sorry! Oh God, I didn't mean to—I didn't know——'

'Dear heaven,' whispered Mike, closing his eyes. Then, pulling her up so sharply that she cried out an involuntary protest, he hauled her quivering body into his arms and buried his face into her hair. A shudder hit his strong, powerful frame, and then he was steady again, like a rock, and he was stroking her hair tenderly, rocking her back and forth. 'You, apologising to me! I'm the one who should be on my knees apologising to you! I was awake the whole time, and I knew you'd try to get away if you could. But I was going to let you get outside and then I was going to follow you, to see what you did. I waited until you got outside and then got dressed, taking my time. Taking my time, dammit!'

He was holding her so tightly, and soothing her, and stroking her, and she clung to him. 'He was k-killing me!' she sobbed. 'I was never so afraid in my life! I couldn't breathe! I——' She gave up trying to talk and just buried her head into his neck and howled. After a few minutes, however, she pushed at his shoulders until she was able to sit up, away from him. She wiped her eyes, grinned a little shakily, and tried to run her fingers through her tangled hair. 'Got a bit out of control there, for a moment.' With huge, deep breaths she was striving to get a grip on her emotions.

He watched her, eyes dark—strangely not green at all, she thought—and a muscle bunched in his tightly clenched jaw. 'It's allowable, you know.'

Her eyes managed to smile at him. 'I know. But I don't like it, all the same. Whenever I cry my eyelids get puffy and I get headaches.'

This made him laugh, reluctantly. 'I've said it once, and I'll say it again, sweetheart, you're something special!' He paused, and a look of what seemed to be pain flitted across his face. 'Promise me something?'

Dee was so tired, too tired. Her head felt as if it weighed ten tons, and her eyelids drooped in spite of herself. She was simply too tired, and sore, and discouraged to fight him any more, and she nodded silently. That made him shake his head ruefully.

'You don't even know what I'm going to ask you.'

'Yes, I do,' she said, sounding like a frog, and she just couldn't help herself as she felt for the pillow behind her and put her head down on it, closing her eyes, so very weary. 'You're going to ask me not to run away until morning. Okay, I won't—too sore and sleepy. Gonna nap first.'

He watched her eyes flutter shut, and when her breathing deepened, he stood to ease her jeans and socks and shoes off, and the sight of her long nightshirt underneath the trim black sweater had him smiling again, but it spoke more of pain than amusement. Then he pulled the covers up and tucked them carefully around her curled-up figure. He sat on the edge of the bed and stroked her hair for some time, looking down at her sleeping, vulnerable, bruised face.

'It wasn't what I was going to ask you,' he whispered quietly. 'But it's good enough for now. It's more than good enough for now.'

CHAPTER FIVE

A SHAFT of sunlight mottled Dee's pillow with a puddle of gold, and she turned her head away in protest. But though she didn't want to, she had already begun to wake up, and she opened her eyes reluctantly to look around her. It was hard to get them open, and with a flash of remembrance, she ruefully realised that she was paying the price for crying last night. Her eyes sought out the other bed and found Mike reading a paperback novel, fully dressed, with his back propped against the headboard and his long legs stretched comfortably out. The bed was made neatly.

Feeling her eyes on him, he turned his head to smile at her. 'Good morning—finally. How are you feeling?' She moved experimentally and winced.

'Sore,' she croaked hoarsely, and put her hand up to her throat in embarrassment. She had forgotten about her bruised larynx. Mike slid off his bed and came over to look at her slim throat carefully, one of his big hands resting casually against the side of her head. Staring up, she saw the dark blue bruise on his cheekbone where he had sustained a blow, and the sudden unexpected terror of last night flooded back with an overwhelming power that made her body quiver. His hand tightened briefly.

'I think that after you use your voice a while, the hoarseness will dissipate,' he said, and his voice and face were so calm and matter-of-fact that she found herself back in control, and grateful for it.

'Oh, probably, but in the meantime I shall sound like a frog croaking,' she whispered, and grinned slightly when he laughed. He continued to laugh, though, without stopping when she would have considered it appropriate to. It had been, she thought, puzzled, a very mild joke. Her eyes narrowed on him as she crossed her legs and looked like a small spirte perched on the huge bed. 'I take it you have a fondness for frogs?' she asked dryly.

Mike sat on the edge of the bed and the springs creaked with his weight. His expression was light, amused ... admiring? Dee wondered at her own perception at that, doubting her own conclusion. His hand was still resting on her, now on her slim shoulder. 'Remind me never to get into a fight with you,' he told her, still chuckling. 'I've taken self-defence courses and consider myself fairly well equipped for whatever might occur, but you! Well, you're something that just isn't in the books. Where did you learn to kick like you did last night? That man went down like a ton of bricks, and he didn't even know what had hit him!'

She chuckled, and it was a dry, painful sound. 'Watching you, I guess. You knocked my feet right out from under me, if my memory serves me right. I don't know, if I'd thought about it, I probably wouldn't have done anything but sit on the ground and have hysterics!'

But he was shaking his head at that, saying, 'No, you wouldn't—you aren't the type to have hysterics. You'd have looked around for something to hit him with. And I'll bet you scarred the other one for life, by the amount of blood you had on you.'

'I certainly hope so,' she said, totally without remorse. She looked down at herself and shuddered with disgust at the dried blood on her sweater. 'He certainly bled like a pig! I need another bath.' A hot one, she thought longingly, and then her expression became more serious, troubled, frightened. 'Mike, why—why do you suppose they attacked me?'

His own expression changed, something dark showing before he carefully masked his features. 'I can only guess,' he replied flatly, running his hand through his hair. 'And I've been doing nothing but guessing all morning. They couldn't have known who you really are—the only people who know that are you and I, and of course your guardians, whom I've kept up to date.' His hand left her shoulder. She found that she missed its weight and she shied away from the thought. 'It could have certainly been a random crime, but they didn't take your bag last night, so I'm afraid they must have had something uglier in mind.' She shuddered convulsively, and his expression gentled. 'Don't dwell on it, though! Nothing irrevocable happened, and you're safe now. But, Dee, we need to talk. There are some things that I'd like to understand better about you before we go anywhere or do anything else. And I think we need to give you a little time to rest up and recover a bit, and let your bruises heal. Can we call a truce? I won't force you to go anywhere, and I won't get in touch with your aunt and uncle for a while. In return, you won't scamper off the very moment I turn my back! And we both know you could do it, too, and get away with it, if only for a while. And we both know, don't we, that I'd come right after you. Something's got to be resolved. Can we trust each other for a while? Can we let things slide a bit?'

She dropped her eyes. His simple words shook her so, and she wanted badly to do what he asked. She wanted to trust him. 'All right. What are we going to do? I'd like to go back home . . .' At her choice of words, his brows shot up and she knew he thought she meant Kentucky. '. . . because I'll bet Mrs Gordon is going out of her mind with worry. And I really should get in touch with my boss, at work.'

Mike had a strange expression on his face. 'Do you really consider that place home?'

Her blue eyes rested on him with sombreness. 'Yes, I do. I've made it my home. I've worked hard and I'd saved money, and I'd wanted to go to college. I decorated that tiny little room with all of the colours I love best . . . yes, it's home to me.'

He was silent for a few minutes, his brows drawn down into a frown and his lips pursed thoughtfully. 'I talked to Mrs Gordon before I left and told her you'd received some rather bad family news, and she doesn't expect you back any time soon. I don't know what your situation at work is like. What do you think you should do?'

'They aren't expecting me back any time soon,' she whispered, and felt suddenly a heavy weight of depression settle on her. 'In fact, Sammy isn't expecting me back at all. He knew the truth about me, you know. When you showed up at the restaurant I wrote him an explanation and said goodbye.' Her face crumpled up into tears as a lost feeling gobbled her up and she said raggedly, 'I guess I don't really belong there, any more. That's the problem, isn't it—I don't belong anywhere—I don't fit in anywhere!' She tried to cross her arms over herself, but was unable to do so, because Mike was there and taking her gently, holding her against his broad comforting, supportive chest. She succumbed to her own need and crept over to sit on his lap, like a child, and her arms slid around the strong column of his warm neck. She just hid her face in his sweater and cried.

After what seemed a very long time, her racking sobs stopped, became controllable again, and her tears dried up. Her breathing came unevenly, in little hiccups, but she was back in touch with reality and no longer dwelling in a well of dark emotion. She felt his hands rubbing her back gently, and his breath stirred her hair. She was in a little cave, made up of his shoulder and neck, and his head rested on the side of hers.

'I got you all wet,' she said, muffled against his neck, her cheek on sodden material.

'I'll dry easily enough,' he whispered back. One hand came up to cup her head, the fingers ruffling her hair and stroking the nape of her neck.

'I'm sorry,' she choked, perilously close to tears again, and wavering back and forth on that line of resistance. It was lamentably low. 'I'm usually in better control than this—I hardly ever cry——'

'Everyone cries now and then, sweetheart. Everybody needs to. Don't apologise for that. Nobody can be strong and tough all the time, not even you, and not even me.' His voice rumbled in his chest, and she could feel the vibrations in her own torso.

'I feel terrible, and I want a bath,' she muttered, taking a deep, unsteady breath. 'And I probably look a horror.'

Mike's face burrowed into her fluffy hair as he chuckled, the movement and the sound so very nice. 'You must be feeling better, then. When a woman thinks of her looks, she can't be too devastated!'

A woman, Dee thought dazedly, he called me a woman. That more than anything made her feel much, much better. She pushed against his chest and surfaced back to the world, knuckling her eyes childishly. Then she peeped out from behind her two hands at him, the blue eyes bright again. That look, from under the golden tousled hair, made her seem elfin, halfwild, and he grinned at the impression.

She in turn saw sparkling green eyes set under straight, heavy brows. His hair was tousled as much as hers and the dark brown waves enchanced his features, the strong, aggressive jaw, the hard crooked nose, that wide forehead. 'If you don't mind, I'm going to take a bath. And if you do mind, I'm going to take a bath,' she said saucily. 'When are we kicked out today?'

'Several hours ago,' he told her, smiling at her look of surprise. 'I've already paid for another day. You were so exhausted I didn't have the heart to wake you earlier.'

'Well then,' she said with satisfaction, swinging her legs out of the bed and sliding off Mike's lap, 'that's settled for now.' She stood and rummaged in her suitcase for a clean set of underwear and clothes, then she headed for the bathroom, sublimely unaware of her bare long legs, the incongruous nightshirt sticking out from a rumpled black sweater. Her hair was ruffled wildly, and Mike's eyes followed her out of the room, his expression strangely soft.

Dee gave a startled, muffled shriek when she saw herself in the mirror. God, what a mess! Running a very hot bath, she sank into it thankfully, bathing briskly and then rinsing with the shower for good measure. She had to wash her hair because of the dried blood, and she grimaced at the tangles that caught in her massaging fingers. Afterwards she dried and dressed in matching blouse and slacks that nearly caught the exact colour of her eyes. Then with her dripping hair hanging down her back, she picked up her nightclothes and padded into the bedroom, grinning at Mike in a mischievous way before dumping her things on her open suitcase. Then she caught sight of herself in the mirror again—and stopped in dismay. The black and blue marks on her neck were appallingly apparent at the open neck of her blouse. The bruise on the side of her head wasn't so bad, for her hair covered most of it and make-up could conceivably do the rest, but those bruises at her throat were shocking in daylight.

Mike was contemplating her with his arms crossed casually at his chest. She noted that he had changed his sweater for a dry one. 'I'm going to have to wear something besides this blouse,' she told him ruefully, gesturing at her throat. 'I hadn't realised how noticeable the bruises are.'

Something dark and violent showed fleetingly in his

eyes before being wiped clean away. 'Yes. They're going to be noticeable for some time, I'm afraid. At least the swelling has gone down.'

She rummaged around in her suitcase and brought up a turtleneck, caramel-coloured sweater, waving it triumphantly at him. 'The solution has been found! Lord, I'm starved—I'll hurry so we can go and eat.' With that she sat off yet again to the bathroom, intent on reaching privacy to change her top, and Mike shook his head mockingly.

'Don't go to the trouble, sweetheart. It's much easier for me to turn my back than for you to wear a path going back and forth to the bathroom all the time.' With that he made good his offer and presented a large, indifferent back for her scrutiny.

Dee hesitated only briefly and then was scrambling out of her blouse and into her turtleneck in two seconds flat. 'Okay,' she mumbled, her mouth hidden in the folds of the sweater, then she was posing in front of the mirror to arrange the neck to her satisfaction. Lean hard fingers came to the back of her neck and lifted out her damp hair, and she muttered a thanks, grinning at how domesticated they looked.

'That's a very provocative grin,' he said in her ear. 'Do you want to share the joke?'

'No,' she gurgled merrily. 'It's a private one.' A hand slapped her bottom smartly.

'That has to mean that I'm the source of your amusement!' he growled. 'How long will it take you to get ready to eat? There's a restaurant right across the highway—if you hurry, I just might let you join me for lunch.'

A blonde brow cocked. 'That's mighty big of you. I'm so flattered at that gracious invitation, I can hardly stand still in one place!'

'Well, so long as you're ready in fifteen minutes, then.'

'I'll be ready in ten.' And she was, brushing her hair one final time in front of the mirror before turning decisively to Mike. He surveyed her cheek, a forefinger under her chin and tilting it up.

'You did a good job with the make-up. It shows only slightly, and only a very observant person would be able to tell there's a bruise.'

He opened the door and lazily lounged by it while she scooted by, tucking her brush into her handbag. Then he was following her, slipping the room key into his pocket.

They opted to walk across the highway instead of taking the car. Dee thrilled to Mike's unexpected touch when he grabbed her hand to drag her into a running dash across the wide stretch of asphalt. She was laughing when they finally slowed on the other side, cheeks glowing and eyes twinkling. For the rest of the walk, he casually draped one arm around her shoulders and they joked and parried swift witticisms.

They were seated immediately and she looked over the menu hungrily. When the waitress came back to take their orders, she let Mike order for her, and soon steaming cups of coffee appeared in front of them both. She watched with a wry lifted eyebrow as the waitress lingered over Mike's cup, her appreciative gaze on him suggestively. He took it very well, leaning back in the booth with a lazy smile that treated the waitress with a warm friendliness that somehow neatly destroyed any sexual connotation that could be construed.

When she finally walked away, Dee raised her cup to him in a mocking salute. 'Well, done, I say,' she murmured. Her hoarseness had dissipated into a rather pleasing huskiness, and she found that talking was no longer painful.

He grinned swiftly at her. 'I thought I'd handled myself quite well too, thank you.'

'I'm sure you've improved with practice!' she retorted laughingly. 'Do you get a lot of attention of that sort?'

'A fair amount,' he countered laconically, his green eyes vivid with his own laughter. Finding him a comfortable and interested companion, she was soon chattering away to him lightly as if she had known him for ever. He was for the most part silent, watching her keenly and shouting with laughter at some of the anecdotes she related about the odd experiences one has when one works in a twenty-four-hour restaurant. She liked to hear his laughter; it was a very pleasing sound.

His attitude seemed to change after a while, and his silence began to have a brooding quality that started to rub on her nerves. She ordered ice cream for dessert and the waitress refilled their coffee cups. After letting the silence fall over them again, Dee finally opened her mouth to ask him about his strange mood when he spoke.

'Strange, isn't it, to be buying a cheap lunch for a millionaire heiress,' he murmured, and there was something odd in his voice and eyes, but she was too shocked with what he said to really notice.

Shock soon gave way to anger, though, and her eyes spat sudden, virulent sparks at him as she hissed, 'Don't you put a label on me, mister! Don't you dare!' She hated the phrase 'millionaire heiress'. As if the only thing about her of value was the money!

'No,' he said consideringly, cocking his head to one side to stare at her with those unsettling, assessing, somehow stern eyes. 'I should be the last to do that, shouldn't I? At every turn you've slipped out of the neat, tidy little mould I've made out for you. You change constantly, like quicksilver, always something new, something unexpected and different. When I'd thought of you as a runaway teenager, you appear to me as a maturing young woman. When I'd labelled you as defeated, you nimbly slip out a second story window to disappear into thin air. Last night, when I'd thought you were beaten, you suddenly strike out with a swiftness and a deadly accuracy that simply floored your opponent. And today,' a slight, uncontrolled smile tugged at one corner of his firm mouth and she stared, fascinated, forgetting her anger, 'today when I'd thought you were perhaps dieting because of the salad you ordered—why, you turn right around and order ice cream!'

The spoonful of chocolate that had been travelling absently to her mouth froze a moment at that, and she stared at it selfconsciously. Chuckling inwardly at his whimsical statement, she stuffed the spoon into her mouth with a robust defiance for the calorie intake, nodding pertly. Mike smiled at her playfulness, appreciatively and yet strangely absentmindedly. There was an underlying seriousness about him, an intent quality that made her suddenly drop her act and sit forward attentively.

'Why did you run away?'

The question was so simply and quietly spoken that for a moment or two it didn't register. When she finally grasped the enormity of the question, her thin face took on a bitterness and a peculiarly hard quality, the eyes shadowing over and the mouth thinning until she looked years older. It was an astonishing change, from her previous lightheartedness to this disillusioned look.

'How long have you got?' she asked him flippantly, the harshness making him wince.

'As long as it takes. I'd like to understand,' he said quietly.

At those mild words, her defiant hostility crumbled and she leaned back in her seat, momentarily at a loss for words. 'I don't know what to say. I've never articulated my reasons to anyone before. Nobody bothered to ask.'

'Try. Was it your aunt and uncle? Did things seem to go wrong when your parents died?'

'I guess you could say that.' She hesitated and a pent-up look filled her eyes. She said, very quietly, 'Have you ever been so very miserable that you just can't take being miserable any more? I mean to the point where, if it was a choice between living in a particular situation or not living at all, you'd choose not to live?'

'No.' He was very attentive.

'I have.' Her simple reply seemed to shake him. 'I had to leave. It was a choice between suicide or leaving home, and I chose the latter because I wasn't quite ready to die yet.' Her bright beautiful blue eyes smiled at him slightly as he looked, stricken, into them. And, because he had asked her, she told him about the barren time, and all her frustrations. She told him about the loneliness, the pressures at college, the feeling of entrapment, everything. She talked with an eloquence born from an urgent need to communicate, and it made Mike sit up.

'You should ask my guardians,' she said conversationally, 'how I did in school, and I'll bet you anything you like that they won't be able to tell you. They don't care. They like the allowance given to them for my support, but bother them with my problems? Don't make me laugh! Do you know, no one remembered my birthday last year? Isn't that rich? That was the breaking point for me. Oh, I'm not talking about birthday presents, gifts, because I had everything materially that I needed or wanted. It's that damned dry emotional desert I was living in that was killing me. Do you hear me, Mike? They were killing me!'

She looked up into his eyes and encountered something brilliant in his green, piercing eyes. There was a curious look about him, as if he were seeing something clearly for the first time and was saddened by what he saw.

He moved, made an effort to speak. 'Wasn't there anyone that you could talk to, turn to, anyone you could ask for help from? Perhaps you were friends with the housekeeper or someone who helped around the house?'

Dee just looked at him blankly. 'I didn't know anyone who worked at the house. Judith got rid of all our employees and hired her own staff.'

'*What?*' It was a thunderous reaction, and Mike shot up straight in his seat as he stared at her, incredulously.

Bewildered, she murmured, 'I suppose you wouldn't have known, but does it really matter now?'

He was staring off into nothing, directing that powerful intellect and attention on to something unseen. He said slowly, 'It may and then again, it may not. Dee, if you were to die, who would inherit the fortune?'

She stared at him, trying to make sense out of an apparently senseless question. 'I'm not sure. I never really considered the possibility of my own death before, I guess, having chosen the other path ... It's probably a classic case of a youth living in the illusion of her own immortality—it's just not something I've thought about. I guess the next of kin would inherit before I turn eighteen, and they still would, if I didn't make a will.'

The words came out slowly from him. 'And Judith and Howard are your next of kin.'

'That's right. They're the only family I have. Everyone else is dead.' It was said simply, as she tried to follow the path of his thoughts, failing dismally.

He said very quietly, 'Oh, my God.' And he stared down at his hands as if he could see blood on them and was sickened by the sight.

'Mike, what is it?' she asked, reaching out and touching one of his hands tentatively. He shook himself like a dog coming out of water, and he looked around as if suddenly realising how long they had sat in the restaurant.

'Let's get out of here,' he muttered, sliding out of the

booth. Still bewildered and yet patient, Dee followed and waited quietly while he paid for the meal. As they walked out of the building, she lagged a little behind and he turned to look at her questioningly.

Her eyes were fixed on the ground. 'Do you suppose I should have stayed and tried to stick things out?' she asked softly, uncertainty hitting her like a huge, consuming wave. 'Do you think I was wrong for wanting to get out from under all that? I always wondered if I was seeing the situation accurately, or if I was just rationalising because I didn't have the guts to stick out a sticky situation.'

His arm came around her, hard, drawing her close, compelling her to walk forward with him over the highway. 'No, sweetheart, I don't think you were wrong,' he said at last, and some of the tension went out of her shoulder blades at his support. It was a strange feeling, this sharing. She wasn't used to it, and she was surprised at how much his approval meant to her. 'It's probably the only thing that saved you.'

Her head turned, and she tried to make sense out of his stern, frowning expression.

Back in the motel room she crossed over to the newly made bed and sank down on to it, her eyes following Mike as he walked over to his suitcase and fingered a shirt aimlessly, his expression never lightening. 'What is it?' she asked at last. 'What's bothering you?'

'I could be wrong,' he murmured, putting a hand to his neck to massage it while he stared at the ceiling. 'It's fantastic. I could be very, very wrong and probably am ... let's forget it for now, all right? Maybe I'll tell you later. I need some time to think.'

'Is—is it about me?'

His head turned at that and he looked at her gently, amusedly. 'Honey, I've thought of precious little except you for the past nine months or so.' And it wasn't the words that he said somehow, but the way that he said them that made her go warm all over, a slow suffusion of happiness that melted into her bones and made her blue eyes gradually take on a shining response.

But the expression died away and she asked in a low voice, 'What do we do now? Where do we go from here? It's funny, but in all the time that I spent running, I—this is the first time I've ever actually felt lost. How long does the truce last, Mike?' Something in her eyes shimmered and she looked quickly down at her hands, lying loosely clasped on her lap.

Footsteps, slow and measured, and then a big warm hand coming lightly to the side of her bent face, running down her neck, under her hair, and then carefully back to cup her tender cheek. She quivered. 'Shall we forget the truce and call it a friendship now?' he asked softly. 'I don't know what to do either, sweetheart, but maybe we can figure something out together. Nothing's quite so hard, if you have someone to share it with. You've been too alone, Dee. Let me shoulder some of the weight for you for a while. I've strong shoulders and a wide back, and I'll respect whatever you ultimately decide. You don't have to run away! I'll help you find what to work towards, instead of forcing you to pick up and run. Can you trust me, just a little bit?'

She turned her face into his hand and whispered, 'I want to!' and felt him bend down to place a kiss on her forehead. Then he stepped back and his hand fell away. He sat on his bed and regarded her wryly, with a quizzical twist to his lips.

'Well then. Instead of a truce with neither of us knowing what to do, now we have a friendship, and neither of us knows what to do!' The statement forced a smile out of her, and her eyes fell away to wander the room idly. They landed on her neat pile of clothes by the suitcase, dirty and bloody.

'You say that you need to think,' she said abruptly. 'I

could use some space, too—why don't we just take the time right here? I'd like to find a laundrymat where I could wash some things,' and she nodded to the corner, making him look. 'I'll bet you have a few things that could stand to be washed too. Let's put off a major decision until this evening or tomorrow, shall we?'

Mike cocked his head at her. 'Such a long time as that!' he mocked, laughing at her flush.

'I make up my mind quickly,' she told him with dignity, 'and lord knows I've had to in the past! I just need a little time to review my options and possible consequences, that's all.'

'Very well.' He stood up. 'Let's do the laundry, then!'

They found a small laundrymat a few miles west, just after driving through a small cluster of blocks with business buildings in a tight group. Dee twisted around in her seat and laughed as she surveyed the street that they had just driven down. 'I'll bet the people here are trying to pass that off as a town!' she giggled, and pointed to the short business district.

Mike pulled into a parking space and turned off the engine, then twisted around to look where she was pointing, a slight smile cocking the corner of his mouth. 'I'll bet you've never lived in a small town before,' he guessed shrewdly, and she shook her head, still laughing. 'Well, I did, and I don't want to hear any more ridicule about the state of small things! In fact, my home town was very like this.'

Dee turned to look at him contemplatively, a smile lurking in the depths of her eyes. 'Typical middle class family,' she guessed. 'With a nice back yard and two dogs. Your father's retired, and you see your parents every Christmas, right?'

His smile turned into a wider grin as he laughed at her. 'You almost got it right. A dog and a cat, and I sometimes go home for Thanksgiving, too.'

'It sounds marvellous. Long summer nights on the back porch swing——'

'—Front porch, but close enough——'

'—and your mother makes nothing but homemade lemonade, right?'

'The best in the country.'

'Where do they live?'

'California—northern, that is. It's a long way away, but I went to college in the mid-West and just seemed to have a natural love of the East. I know where home is, though, and I drop in once in a while, for the occasional dose of serenity. It's good enough for me.' His smile held a wealth of remembered love and happiness in it, and Dee suddenly felt saddened and didn't know why.

'Well!' she said, suddenly brisk. 'We'd better get our clothes started, hadn't we?' And she opened her car door, only to be stopped by Mike's hand, heavy and detaining on her slim arm.

As she looked an enquiry, he said, 'Dee, promise me something, please. Don't go anywhere by yourself, all right? Stick close to me today.'

Her eyes widened with hurt and surprise. 'But why? You still don't trust me, do you? You still think I'll try to get away.' There was pain in her voice and midriff as bewilderment clouded her mind at his strangely urgent request.

'No!' he said sharply, shaking her arm a little. 'No, Dee. Please—I'll explain later, if I may, but just don't go off by yourself. We can't talk here and it's too complicated, and I don't even know if I'm right or wrong. I'm—worried about you. Just try to trust me a little, too, okay?' His hand left her arm and without physically touching her, he still held her with his eyes.

She had to close hers. 'I don't understand,' she whispered, 'but I'll do it.' Then she opened her eyes and stared at him hard. 'But I think you'll have a lot of explaining to do later.'

He seemed to relax, and he nodded at her. 'I will.' And his words had a certain promising ring to them that she just had to believe. They went into the laundrymat, both engulfed in their own thoughts.

Dee slowly deposited the clothes into the washing machine, her mind awhirl with chaotic thoughts. So much had happened in the past few days! She knew her life would never be the same again, and it was all because of Mike. Despite every logical reason for her to doubt him and be wary, every instinct and intuition in her tugged towards trusting him. It was a war of intellect and intuition that was being waged within her, and she felt torn apart.

She didn't feel she could gracefully and happily go back to Kentucky, and she had expressly given her promise to Mike that she wouldn't run away again without consulting him. So what were her options, really? She had to confess to an almost overwhelming desire to go back to Kentucky, in spite of all the heartache she knew she would encounter there, and she was honest enough to know that the reason was Mike. He lived in Kentucky, probably quite close to where her home was. It seemed that anything she decided contrary to going home would mean that she would probably never see him again, for all his protestations of friendship. She didn't know if she thought beginning in a new location would be worth it.

She didn't know what to do.

Her troubled face lifted at a quick touch to her shoulder. Mike had gone to the counter to buy soap and get change, and he handed it to her silently, his eyes questioning. Dee smiled and shook her head, dumping the soap into the machine and stepping back so that he could put coins into the slot. The machine churned to life, and he turned to the row of chairs available, only to look back as she didn't join him.

She grinned. 'I'm going to find the little girls' room,'

she told him, and made her way to the back hall as he found a seat. The hall was behind the counter with the bored lady attendant leafing through magazines, and Dee nodded to her as she passed. There was an exit door in the back marked 'Fire Exit Only', standard for public buildings, and she noticed that it was standing wide open. That was not quite so usual, and she called back to the lady at the counter, 'Hey! Did you know your fire exit is standing wide open?' There was no answer, at least none that she could hear, and she started to walk back down the tiny hall to call again. 'Hey! Did you know——'

And someone grabbed her roughly from behind, interrupting her call and making her scream, more from surprise and outrage than any particular fear. Then things started to happen very fast. She heard Mike's shout and the sound of running feet, and she started to struggle wildly, but the person behind her knew what he was doing and held her arms to her sides. She noticed a bandage on his left hand, and realisation struck her, so terrifyingly and suddenly that she didn't seem to have any breath at all. Then she found her voice and screamed again, piercingly, and someone slapped her so hard she felt blood burst from her lip. Through pain-glazed eyes she saw the other man with a small black thing in his right hand—a gun! He seemed to be waiting, and she heard Mike's deep, concerned shout.

'Dee! Dee, are you all right . . .?'

'Mike!' she screamed, 'don't come back here, they have a gun——'

Then the man hit her again and she grunted as her world exploded into white-hot sparks, and just as she faded into blackness she heard another shout and the sharp, deadly report from that ugly black gun. Mike, her mind cried out, anguished—oh, God!

CHAPTER SIX

A RED, moving darkness. A red, moving, purring darkness, and Dee stirred, sighed and opened her eyes. But she saw nothing but the red woollen blanket that was pulled over her, making her world dark. Something painful jutted into her hip. She was on the floor of a moving car, lying right across the exhaust hump, bouncing with every bump in the road. The car jolted and she winced with the pain. She was going to be very bruised on her left hip. She moved tentatively and found that her hands and feet were bound tightly. She couldn't feel her hands, and that made brief, frustrated tears blur her vision for a moment.

A sudden strange, male voice just in front of her said, 'D'you think she's awake yet?'

Another strange voice answered, 'Dunno. I'll look.' And she made her face and body go completely, utterly limp, effective out of sheer desperation and fear. The blanket was lifted and there was silence for a moment, then the blanket fell on her. 'She's out cold. You hit her pretty hard.'

'Yeah—well, she was screeching like a banshee. I had to do something to make her stop since you were too afraid to put your hand over her mouth.' There was a sneer in the voice.

The second man answered indignantly, 'Could you really blame me? The little bitch sank her teeth into me that last time so hard I had to have stitches! Besides, I didn't see you handle that guy with any degree of efficiency. Did you have to shoot him, for God's sake? I'll bet what happened today will be all over the newspapers tomorrow. So much for being quiet about the whole thing!'

'Shut up!' It was a quiet snarl that sent chills down Dee's spine. The other man subsided, muttering, and they went on for a while in silence.

Mike! she cried silently, and then the tears came, large and wet, splashing on to the floor and soaking into the carpet. She couldn't comprehend what was happening. She couldn't comprehend Mike dead. She got a sudden, horrifying vision of his big, vital body lying in a growing puddle of his life's blood, and had to swallow down a growing wave of nausea and grief. Then with short, silent shallow pants she forced herself to get under a grim control. She would cry for Mike later and then try to understand why his death made her feel so utterly desolate, but right now she had to concentrate on the present moment, and survival.

She was in such a dazed state of shock and grief that at first she didn't pay attention to what was being said. Gradually, though, she realised that the men in front were speaking again, and she forced herself to listen to the conversation.

'. . . almost there,' the first one was speaking.

'It's the next turn left. No hope of making it look like an accident, not with those marks on her face and neck,' the second man said.

Shock coursed through her so violently she felt her heart jump in her chest. Those two men were talking about killing her as easily as if they were discussing the next Sunday picnic! Why was this happening to her? What did they want? Horrible visions flitted through her mind, chasing each other like nasty little ogres, of what could happen to a young and defenceless girl. Panic welled up in her, crowding at the back of her throat like a pent-up scream, beating at her temples. She fought it, but tears continued to drip down her nose, falling wetly off the tip. Oh, Mike, where are you? I *need* you——

The car's motion slowed, then slewed left, and she snapped back to the danger so imminent. Scrubbing her face into her shoulder to try to dry her face, she listened as the first man said, 'You haul her out while I open the door. You're sure this place is empty?'

'Yeah, the family's on vacation. It was a stroke of luck hearing that in the doctor's office. The house is nicely secluded, too. Nobody around to hear.'

Nobody around to hear . . . The car stopped and doors slammed and opened, and Dee felt her senses whirl as she was hoisted on to a rough shoulder. She went as limp as a piece of string, breathing shallowly, eyes closed. She was jolted around for a bit and then it seemed that she was carried up a flight of stairs and thrown down on something soft. The footsteps receded and a door closed. She heard the scrape of a lock.

Cautiously she opened her eyes and looked around her. She was alone. With a little more bravery, she lifted her head and surveyed the bedroom she had been deposited in. The bed was a single one, and the room fairly small. She noted the stuffed animals on the waist-high dressing table and guessed it must be a child's room. Tremblingly, she attempted to sit up, but fell back, so she tried again and this time managed to make it up. With a heavy heart and absolutely no will to do much of anything, she stared at the tape wound around her slim ankles and her chin quivered. Mike.

Then her gaze sharpened. *Tape?* Sure, it could hold someone well enough if plenty were used, but there wasn't anything easier to cut through. Looking around with more interest, she started to think of what she could use on the tape when something scraped outside the door. She threw herself back down, but didn't have to worry, since no one came into the room. The men were doing something, bumping around and making noise, and she heard sounds of an argument. Then someone walked by the room, and she heard him call

out, '. . . get the job done, then, and get the hell out of
here . . .' The other called back something, but was too
far away for her to hear well enough, and the gist was
lost to her.

The sounds of someone moving around faded, and
she lifted up her head to search the room for reachable
sharp things, her intention to try and get loose from her
bonds. She soon had to give up. The room was too
solidly child-proofed. She turned her face into the
bedspread to keep the yellow afternoon sun from
blinding her and, amazingly, slept.

Drowsy. She turned her head and winced awake as
the soreness of her neck muscles twanged painfully. She
looked to the window and found the sky greying into
late afternoon. How long had she slept? Then she
twisted around and stared at her bluish, numbed,
useless hands. They were lifeless, but her feet weren't so
lucky. Knife-like needles from abused nerve endings
made her squirm. She thought back over what the one
man had said. They had some kind of job to do. What
was it? A faint drifting smell of smoke made her nose
twitch and she shook her head. Another, stronger whiff
of smoke assailed her quivering nostrils. She wondered
briefly at the stupid person who was burning rubbish on
a dry day like today—then she froze into utter
immobility. The window was tightly closed. The smoke
was not coming from outside. The smoke was coming
from within.

The house was on fire.

She was in the house, trapped as efficiently as could
be, with no possible hope of escaping this one. After the
first shock of knowledge, she subsided tiredly. What
difference did it make? Chances were good that it
wouldn't hurt. Most people died from smoke inhalation,
not from actually burning to death. She was just too
discouraged and tired to fight any more. What did it
matter? Mike was dead.

She turned her face into the soft bedspread that was decorated with grinning cartoon figures and waited patiently.

She never could really remember that much about the time she waited for the smoke to get too bad for breathing. She knew that she looked sometimes out the window at the darkening sky, and sometimes she looked at the small crack of space between the door and the floor, watching for the deadly white curls of nothingness that would snuff out her life.

It came amazingly quickly. She stared at the first thin tendrils, thinking that the two men must have laid the fire very well for it to catch so soon. Then the smoke was coming in thicker and thicker and she started to cough, the acrid smell burning her throat and making her eyes water copiously—or was she crying for Mike and for herself, and for the life that she never would properly finish?

Then she could hear the noise, the roaring, ferocious noise of the mindless monster that crept relentlessly to the sky, eating wood and home and girl as it went. She wondered fuzzily if her teeth would tell anyone who she really was, or if she would be buried in an anonymous grave, all shrivelled and charred and brittle. She shivered convulsively, unable to imagine the total non-existence of that personality the world called Dee . . .

' . . . Dee! . . . are you, for God's sake? . . . Deirdre? Dee, dammit, are you here? . . . Where are you, girl?'

She turned her head a little on the bedspread, coughed, and wondered if she was hallucinating the sound of Mike's voice hoarsely, desperately calling her name over and over. She must be mad.

'Dee, for God's sake, tell me where you are!'

Her head snapped up. That was no hallucination. That was a full-throated roar of fear and dread and rage and—that was Mike.

'Mike!' she screamed. 'I'm up here! Oh, God, they

said they shot you and I thought you were dead and I'm so scared up here—*Mike!*

'Keep calling, Dee, I'll be right there—don't give up . . .'

She heaved right off the bed and landed as hard as she could contrive, making quite a satisfactory thump. Then she twisted to her back, ignoring the screaming protest from her jerked and abused shoulder muscles, and kicked the floor as hard as she could, a steady rhythm of life and hope and desperation pounded on that naked floor. The floorboards were warm. The panic that hadn't come when she had been hopeless came then, a wave of pure terror, and she screamed for Mike, crying.

Over the steady and inhuman roar from the insidious, white-hot fire, she heard pounding footsteps in the hall then they stopped. 'Dee!' Mike shouted. 'Which room?'

'Here!' she sobbed. The handle turned, rattled, and something heavy slammed into the wood. She heard herself, quite detached in a way, as she sobbed out a steady stream of hysteria. 'Yes! Yes! Oh, God, get me out of here—please just get me out of here——'

The door splintered open and he surged in, his dark hair falling like black rain over a grim brow, his eyes glittering like precious stones, his mouth pulled into a grimace revealing white teeth. One second and he was heaving a broad, panting chest in a great sigh, staring at her crouched on the floor staring at him, and the next second he was down beside her, hauling her up against him hard, his mouth all over her face, raining shaking, fierce, thirsting kisses, and she could barely feel them, because she was kissing him back, anywhere she could reach him—his jaw, his cheek, his brow and then his lips.

And his lips were crushing hers, drinking, giving, hurting and the hurt was so deliciously wonderful, so wonderfully alive, she welcomed the pain. He pulled back, set her on her feet, and she promptly began to fall, crying out. Mike jerked her into his arms and deposited her on the bed, wrenching at the tape around her ankles and ripping it off within a few seconds, then reaching behind her. 'Sorry, I didn't notice . . .'

'Oh, darling——' she gasped out an unsteady, unamused laugh. She couldn't feel his fingers. 'It won't do any good. I won't be able to walk—the circulation has been cut off too long——' The tape was off her wrists, for her shoulders were suddenly eased from their cramped confinement, and she brought her hands around to touch them together tentatively. Nothing.

'Not to worry, my love,' he said, sounding incredibly calm after his ferocious bellowing. 'I'll carry you. You can't be much of a load, such a little thing, after all. I'll just sling you up over my shoulder like so, and we'll be off——' He started out of the door and down the hall, carrying her, contrary to his words, tightly against his chest, shielding her nose and mouth. They were forced back into the room as red angry flames licked wickedly at the stairs. The roar of the monster was nearly a scream.

Mike shoved at the door with one foot and went to the window after dumping her on the hateful bed, weak and frightened, tears streaming down her face. He tried the window, found it nailed shut, so he found something to wrap around his forearm and smashed it right through the glass, running his padded arm around the edges to be sure all the dangerous jagged edges were broken off. Then he surveyed the outside for a brief moment, and looked back at Dee. He had apparently made up his mind, and he strode over to sweep her on to the floor, laughing recklessly down into her face.

'Didn't I tell you not to worry?' he mocked, kissing her hard.

She smiled at him quaveringly, trying to joke, 'I'm sorry, I've just had a bad day.'

His eyes softened on her unbelievably, then he was moving swiftly, tearing up sheets from the small bed with a rippling flex of his shoulders, tying the pieces together in an amazingly short amount of time. He tied one end to the bedpost, yanking the bed over to the window and throwing the other end out. It disappeared with a snaking slither.

He turned back to Dee and wordlessly held out his arms. She rose to her knees and wrapped her arms tightly around his neck, pressing kisses against his jawline and ear. She felt him kiss her back, then he carried her to the window. 'It's only the second story, love. Do you think you could keep those lovely arms around my neck for that long, hmm?'

She drew back, stammering, 'My hands—I can't hold on to anything——'

He drew one finger down the side of her cheek. 'I won't let you fall.' And looking into his wonderfully sparkling, vividly alive eyes, she believed him. She tightened her arms around his neck and he wrapped one arm securely around her waist, swinging them both over the windowsill. Then they were dropping into the air, Mike's neck and shoulder muscles bunching painfully, straining, as he lowered them both to the ground.

Once down and feeling the incredible destructive heat that had not yet broken through the outside wall, Mike hauled Dee up into his arms and carried her swiftly away from the burning, dying house. She held on to him and buried her face into his hard, warm, moving shoulder. Some distance away, he stopped and lowered her on to the hood of a car. Her head surfaced briefly. It was his dark green sedan. She buried her face again into him, feeling the marvellously good texture to his skin, smelling his scent, touching him and being held.

He pulled away. 'Dee darling, we've got to call the fire department so that they can get this blaze under control or the whole wood will burn. Are you all right, dear girl?' The tender tone and the slightly unsteady hand that passed through her hair made her gulp, and she nodded, waveringly. He scooped her up and put her gently into the car, grabbing a soft comforter from the back and tucking it under her. Then he swiftly got into the driver's side and reversed down the driveway with a squealing of tyres. Just as they reached the road and he turned right, a distant wailing siren was heard. Mike slowed and pulled off the road, cocking his head and listening intently and Dee peered down the road briefly, but uninterestedly, because her hands and feet were coming alive with a painful intensity. Several red-flashing, wailing trucks passed by, and Mike relaxed, sighing. 'Well, they got here quicker than if we'd had to call, didn't they?' His head rested wearily on the headrest and he turned his head to look at her. 'What is it, sweetheart? Are you hurt after all?'

Dee turned her face away as the tears streamed down her face. The pain was becoming unbearable, and she shifted restlessly to ease it, but moving only made it worse. 'It's my hands and feet,' she muttered, as he pulled her close to him again. 'I'm not hurt, but—but they're on fire, and they prick so painfully, and—that's all. It's silly to cry, and I've cried so damned much, it seems, but—Mike, I thought you were dead! I thought you were dead!'

And of all the many experiences of the day, the terrifying, the infuriating, and the very good, what she remembered most about it was the darkened early evening when she sobbed out her pain and tiredness and deep relief into the living warmth of Mike's arms, smelling pungent smoke in her hair and clothes on a fiery dark and red, balmy night. The sounds of sirens wailed mournfully in the distance and an unseen hand stroked her hair.

She wasn't exactly sure when she fell asleep, but she remembered Mike tucking her carefully into her corner and the car starting up with a gentle purr. She remembered the passage of time and space, the wind whistling through Mike's slightly cracked window. She remembered his stern, drawn face, half obscured by darkness and occasionally lit up into brilliance by the passage of bright, glaring cars. She dozed and then remembered the car stopping and him sliding out of the car. That was when she cried out and reached for him with both urgent hands, and he soothed her patiently, telling her he would be right back. Then he disappeared for a time and sounds came to her of the boot opening and closing. Then he was back as he'd promised, but Dee was so deeply asleep by that time that she never even stirred when he bent over to kiss her and tuck a corner of the blanket under her feet.

She slept on and on and finally woke to sit up and look bewilderedly around. It was pitch black outside, the black of the dead of night, with icy white sparkling stars winking overhead. Mike's face was impassive and unfathomable in the faint glow of the lit dashboard. She glanced at him, at the unending strip of road that the car's speed ate up avidly. Finally she looked back at him in time to see him send her a quick, unexpressive gaze. 'We're on an interstate highway, aren't we?' she asked him quietly.

He nodded. She glanced around again, and what little scenery that she could make out appeared to be that found in northern Kentucky. She turned her puzzled, questioning gaze back to Mike, but he said nothing.

A myriad collection of thoughts danced through her mind, uppermost the dread of going back to that homeless house, the uncaring hostility, the remembrance of Mike as being the hunter, the pursuer, the enemy. Then she recalled his gentleness to her, his understanding. She thought of him asking for her trust. Then she deliberately emptied her mind of all thought and stretched out to put her head against his thigh as a pillow, curling her legs comfortably. She could feel his eyes on her, could feel his mind wondering at his reaction, and she turned her head to smile at him sleepily.

'Wherever we're going, wake me when we get there,' she murmured. 'Unless, of course, you'd like me to drive. In that case, I don't vouch for your safety or the continued existence of this car unscathed!' She giggled a bit, then snuggled her cheek down to his warm leg. She could feel his tension and wondered what he was thinking.

Mike gave a sigh and relaxed. 'You'd be more comfortable if you stretched out in the back,' he said softly. She put her hand lightly on his knee.

'No. Would you like me to move? I will if you're uncomfortable.'

He answered as simply. 'No. Oh no.' A hand descended to her shoulder and squeezed briefly, then was put back on the steering wheel. 'You stay right there. Thank you, Dee.'

She burrowed into the softness of the blanket, feeling the delicious contrast between its yielding pliancy and the hardness of his leg muscle. 'You're welcome.' And again she slept, fitfully, waking sometimes to his hand resting lightly on her neck.

Some time later the car's motion changed, and she stirred. Mike was pulling off the highway and he said tersely, 'Lie still a moment. I don't want to knock your head.' She kept down while he negotiated the turn, then she eased away from him to look around her with blurred eyes.

'Are we there yet?' she asked, voice fuzzed by sleep.

She heard his low chuckle and glanced at him in time to catch the fleeting whiteness of his smile in the semi-darkness. 'Dear, sweet, patient thing—you don't even know where "there" is, do you? No, we aren't there, I just can't drive any more without the fear that I might nod off as I stare at those lovely white lines on the road that flash on and on.'

'I could drive,' she mumbled, and sank against the car door to close her eyes.

'We're not that desperate,' he replied dryly, his exhaustion running through his amusement. 'We're going to get a room and sleep until we wake on our own. You've had it and so have I.'

They pulled into the parking lot of a roadside motel that was still open, and Dee stumbled out along with him. He stopped and stared at her. 'Go back and stay in the warm car until I call for you,' he urged, shooting out a hand as she staggered.

She doggedly shook her head. 'I want to come with you.' She blinked as she looked around. She didn't want to stay in the car by herself. Silly, probably, but there it was. She followed him and didn't even notice his tired grin at her appearance. She was totally unaware that she still had the blanket around her and that she was peering from it like a small street urchin wrapped in rags, reeking of smoke. His arm went around her shoulders bracingly, and she leaned against him as if it was the most natural thing in the world to do.

Later, after they had carried in their luggage, Mike locked the door and he turned to one of the two beds, stripping off his clothes with the simple economy of movement that bespoke overwhelming exhaustion, and an overriding desire to get in between the sheets despite clothes flung on the floor and chair. Clad in only his briefs and unaware of Dee's riveted and fascinated gaze at the sleek animal beauty of his long body, he slipped between the covers and settled with a sigh on the pillows. Greatly tired herself, in spite of her sleep snatched in the car, she also stripped right there, uncaring if Mike's attention was on her or not. It just didn't seem to matter. She slid a clean nightshirt over her head, yawning so widely that her jaw cracked, and started at the unexpected sound of Mike's voice, sleepy and amused, 'You look about twelve years old in that thing.'

She grinned as he stretched luxuriously, hugely, and she padded over to turn out the light with a careless flick of her wrist. Then, suddenly paralysed by the thought and the totally unexpected emotional need that struck at her, she stood motionless in the middle of the dark room. A spasm of shaking swept through her as she stood, chilled and alone.

A rustle of sheets. 'Dee?' he asked her quietly, the deep timbre of his voice luring her more than he could know. 'Why are you just standing there like that? Is something wrong?'

Slowly, very slowly, she advanced until her leg brushed the side of his bed. She trembled, wondering what he would think if she just slipped into his bed. Dared she? A hesitant, trembling hand went questing out and found a corner of sheet. Just to slip in beside him and to be held, so wonderfully close and warm and safe. What if he rejected her? What if he turned away?

His voice came again, puzzled, patient and very, very tired. 'Dee? Where are you? I can't see in this infernal darkness. Are you all right, love?'

And at that she suddenly knew. She pulled back the coves with a sureness as solid as a rock, and slid right in, encountering long, warm, hard legs with her own slighter, cold ones. She pulled the covers over herself as she felt the quiver of shock run through him. The warmth of his body was like an electric heater and yet so much more enticing and comforting, for it was living and breathing and able to give her what she needed.

'God——' he muttered, as if it were jerked out of him, '——Dee, what are you doing?'

'Trying to get warm,' she whispered, and another

spasm of chills shuddered through her. 'I'm being selfish, you see. I want to be held, and warmed, and I want to go to sleep knowing that when I wake up I won't be alone. I don't want to be alone, Mike.' Her voice trailed away to a mere thread of sound.

Utter stillness and then, convulsively, his arms slid around her, drawing her close to his long, warm, vibrant body. She snuggled and cuddled and drew as close as she could, and there wasn't anything sexual at all between them—and yet curiously enough there was. Just to know that Mike was so definitely, exquisitely, alienly male made the warmth very interesting indeed. He groped and searched for her hands and found them carefully tucked away from him, as cold as ice. He pulled them close, in spite of her tentative tugs, and laid them right against the heat of his chest without so much as a flinch. It felt so wonderful and so incredibly good to her, like the rest of his body, that she sighed, relaxing, and she felt him relax too. He drew her head on to his shoulder and she found that it fit just exactly right in the hollow of his neck and shoulder muscles. A quick, slight movement had her pressing her soft lips against the side of his neck and then relaxing again.

'Thank you, Mike.'

'You're very welcome, Dee.'

They slept.

Delicious warmth and the total relaxation of tired, sore muscles. Dee turned her head, murmured in her sleep, and roused a bit at the light that peeped through the thin slots of curtain across the room. She stretched her legs lazily and collided with longer, harder, smoothly muscled legs. Freezing in surprise, she remembered and relaxed again. She slid close to Mike's warmth and started to drift off to sleep again, after briefly and uninterestedly wondering what time of morning it was. A large, questing hand roused her as it touched her bare thigh, and she murmured, 'It's just me.'

A low, husky voice vibrated through her back as he slid closer. 'Hmm, so I've found. How could I have forgotten? Good morning.'

'Mm, g'morning.' Dee froze again as that roving hand crept slowly along her rib cage, over her slim shoulder to the hair that lay on her neck. The hair was brushed gently aside and warm lips pressed to her nape. The pure physical delight that quivered through her at this was totally new and unexpected, and she melted right to the bone at his touch, sighing.

The hand quested down again, found the edge of her nightshirt, slipped in. 'Dee,' it was said very, very softly, and yet she still caught the quiver of something ragged running through it. The hand stilled a moment, fingers tightening, lying heavily and yet gently against her ribs. 'You'd better get out of this bed right now. Please, get out.'

He was saying two different things, she thought hazily. He was asking her to stay with his hands and telling her to go with his words. And she found that she wanted to stay so very much, and with a rightness and a completeness, she realised why she wanted to stay.

Of course she loved him. She had known yesterday, underneath, when she'd been overwhelmed with desolation at the thought of him dead. She had known at the bursting of joy when she had heard him calling her name over the sound of the fire. She had known when Mike had pulled her close yesterday, and held her.

She turned in his arms and looked at him clearly, letting him see the emotion and the desire in her eyes, without prevarication, and the smile that she gave to him was like the morning sun rising and spilling its brilliance over a darkened countryside. She heard him catch his breath and felt him come up on one elbow to stare down at her. 'Can you look me in the eyes and tell me straight to my face that you want me to leave?' she asked him softly, feeling somehow much more controlled than he at the moment. 'Because if you can, I'll go, but not before then.'

His eyes dropped to her moving lips, then he closed them and swallowed. 'No matter what happens?' he muttered, his hand clenching convulsively.

She touched him and felt the reverberations of her touch shudder through his entire length. 'Especially for what would happen,' she whispered.

His eyes opened and he stared deeply into her eyes, the green vivid, violent, leaping, fringed with lovely long lashes under a dark and heavy brow, cleanly moulded. His head gradually lowered to her, his eyes never leaving hers, and her heart started a slow, hard pounding that threatened to stop her ears with its roar. He was leaning over her and his lips hovered over hers. She saw his eyes flutter shut. Just before he kissed her, he whispered, 'I can't.'

CHAPTER SEVEN

DEE woke again and smiled involuntarily. To be held and to be warm and to be loved—what more could one want out of life? A heavy weight lay on her legs and on her waist, and she had her right hand curled in Mike's hair at the back of his head. She turned to look at him and he was so close that all she had to do was reach out just a little with her lips. She did, and at her light, feathery touch he awoke too, kissing her back, eyes closed and a low, deep, husky groan of satisfaction purring in his throat. The heavy weight on her legs moved as he shifted his, and the weight at her waist tightened deliciously, but he was rolling away to lie on his back.

'Good morning again. You're a wonderful sight to wake up to,' he murmured, head turned on the pillow, smiling lazily at her. Dee stretched and moaned as she felt the creak of sore, abused muscles. Memory flooded her, and she raised a selfconscious hand to her face.

'Beautifully black and blue, no doubt,' she said wryly, laughing at him laughing at her. 'I was having the most wonderful dream.'

'Oh?' he murmured, coming up on one elbow and running a long finger down her nose. 'And what were you dreaming about?'

'About this warm and sensitive man I met a few days ago,' she replied softly, reaching up to his face. He turned his head and kissed her fingers. 'We were running around and around, and he was chasing me. He finally caught me, too, and when we looked back at where we'd been running, we found we'd been going in crazy circles, and not only had he been after me, but I'd

118

been after him. Then there was this huge, roaring monster that chased us all over the place and it started to rain. The rain melted all our clothes off . . .'

'Dee?' he questioned softly, a white smile touching his firm lips. She stopped to look up at him, eyes wide and innocent. 'Are you making this up as you go along?'

She nodded, mischief in her eyes, and he started to laugh. 'But,' she hastened to tell him, 'I did meet a warm and sensitive man a few days ago.'

'Oh, you did?' He bent his head and began to trail a line of tiny kisses from her neck to her shoulder, up to her mouth for a long, long while, and then back again. 'Do I happen to know this person? I'm not sure if I entirely approve of you making friends that easily with a total stranger . . .'

'Of course you know him,' she whispered into his ear, pressing a kiss to his jaw and feeling the roughness of his unshaven face. He nuzzled her, then stopped still as she continued blithely, 'You remember Chuck, the trucker, don't you?'

And she shrieked with devilment and laughter as he tightened two warning hands on her with a mock-serious growl of anger. After a few more minutes of this kind of play, Mike slapped her hip and said with a sigh, 'I'll bet it's some ungodly time of day and we should have been up hours ago. It's time you and I were out of bed, my girl.'

He slid out of the covers and stood, a quick, fluid movement, and as she stared at the smooth strength of his muscular body, she went warm with remembrance. He was turning to look at her, though, and she ducked under the covers again, giggling. One seeking hand came under the covers in search of her, and she slapped at it. 'No, I won't! The bed's too warm—ow! All right—all right! I'll get out, for heaven's sake, just stop tickling me! You wombat, I'll bite if you don't let go of

me—oof!' That last was as he scooped her up high into
his arms, swung her around in a dizzying circle, and
deposited her in a heap on the crumpled bed. Her hair
went flying and her legs were all tangled up in a heap,
and her eyes were such a vivid, brilliant, flashing blue,
they captured his attention and held him still. She was
laughing up at him as he towered over her, and as he
watched, her smile slowly died away to leave a more
serious, perplexed pucker around the eyes.

Dee stared at him, feeling all the questions and the
incomprehensions of the previous day well up inside
her. The questions she had been too exhausted, too
overwhelmed, too drained to ask herself last night now
clamoured for attention. 'Mike, about yesterday—I
don't understand any of it. I don't see why those men
came after me in broad daylight. It—it doesn't make
sense, does it?' And the look in her eyes as she stared at
him was lost, bewildered, and somehow imploring.

Something clicked over in his face, something slight,
undefinable, and so tangibly real that she stared,
harder. It was, inexplicably, a barrier. 'What don't you
understand, love?' he asked calmly, sitting on the bed.

Puzzlement quivered through her. 'Well ... for
instance, why do you suppose those two men abducted
me after attempting to and failing the night before?
Once might be a random incident, but twice? Come on,
now, really——'

His jaw clenched, briefly, and she sensed the smoky
embers of a deep anger that had not quite died down
yet. 'I expect because they were afraid you'd seen them
the night before and wanted to get rid of you before
you identified them and pressed charges,' he replied
smoothly.

'But it was nearly pitch black that night!' she
protested against this line of reasoning. It seemed
illogical. 'I didn't even get the slightest hint of what
they looked like.'

'But you marked one of them quite definitely with that nasty bite of yours,' he pointed out, after a moment's reflection.

Dee nibbled at a finger thoughtfully, frowning. 'That's true. But it still seems a bit much, don't you think?' He didn't answer, and after a moment she shrugged fretfully. 'Oh, well, it's over now, and it doesn't matter any more! But it's still strange, and it makes me wonder. One of them said something about having a job to complete, and I never have figured that one out. Oh, and I know that the house they found was totally by chance. One of them had overheard in the doctor's office about it being vacant.'

'There,' said Mike immediately. 'That's your answer. The job they had to complete must have been robbing the house.' She stared at him.

'That hadn't occurred to me,' she said slowly. 'I suppose it's possible. By the way, however did you manage to find me so conveniently in the nick of time?'

'I'd managed to dive into my car and follow them a ways,' he said, smiling crookedly. 'But then I managed to lose them in the residential area where that house was. The streets are very winding and confusing, and I was sweating out a whole host of fears before I finally noticed a whiff of smoke coming from the house you were in. It was hidden from the road, and I'd gone up on the driveway purely out of a rather hopeless curiosity, wondering who in their right mind would be burning trash on a day like yesterday.'

'How very strange,' she murmured. 'It was my thought exactly, before I realized the house was on fire. Then, of course, everything made sense.'

He said dryly, 'Of course. Anyway, I noticed it was the house, too, and then went to the front door to see if anyone was at home. The lock, I saw, had been forced and I became suspicious enough to break inside. I called for you, experimentally, and you answered. The rest is history.'

'Well!' she said, laughing in a way that was not amused at all. 'Am I glad you're of an inquisitive nature! Otherwise I'd be past history right now.' And a shudder quivered through her shoulders at the cold, frightening thought.

Mike was suddenly brisk. 'Come on, up now for sure. We have a lot to do today, and more of our journey yet to go. Hurry, or I'll lay first claim to the shower and use all the hot water!' Dee smiled, reluctantly, but something niggled at the back of her mind, even as she obediently rose to pad into the plain white bathroom and turn on the taps. She couldn't pinpoint the problem, not even to herself, for she wasn't sure she'd correctly picked up the unspoken messages Mike emitted.

The slight impression that something was not quite right haunted her throughout their quickly snatched meal, in a restaurant not far from the motel where they had stayed. Mike was responsive enough to her conversation, and yet she noticed his eyes straying to the window when he thought she wasn't looking. He smiled quickly enough at her jokes and good humour, and it didn't seem to reach his eyes. He responded quickly to her outstretched hand, tucking his big, warm one into hers, and yet it was done with a sombre expression that had her more than a little worried.

She helped carry the suitcases to the car later on, watching him covertly. After he had taken the key to the front office while she waited in the car, she saw him come out of the building slowly and stop, his head turned to the road south, away from her, the spring breeze fluttering through his dark hair. The set to his shoulders was stiff. Then he moved, breaking the brief illusion that she had felt when he had stood so absolutely still, like a marble statue, no feeling and no expression on his face. When he got into the car and put the key to the ignition and yet made no move to start the car, she finally spoke.

'What's wrong?' She watched him, worried. Silence, no movement, no indication that he had heard her. 'Mike, something's been troubling you all day long. What is it? Where are we going? Why aren't you talking to me?'

The questions were spoken quietly, and she tried to sound placid enough so that he would know that she was not worried and trusted him, but something quivered through her words despite her efforts. He didn't turn to look at her and his hand went out to the ignition. The car purred to life. 'What do you mean, I haven't been talking to you? I've been talking to you all day long,' he replied expressionlessly. Dee jerked in her seat.

'No, you haven't. You've been making surface noises to appease me. You haven't really said anything *to* me since we got out of bed. Is—is it me? Is it something I've said, or—or done?' Her voice wobbled betrayingly at the end, and she caught her breath, furious at herself for showing such distress at his uncommunicative mood.

Out of the corner of her eye she saw him glance sharply at her unsteady voice, and his hand flashed out, caught hold of her fingers and gripped them so tightly it hurt. She held on to the pain as if it were a reassurance, which in a way it was. 'You're referring to last night and this morning, I take it,' he said quietly. Dee stared out of her window blindly and nodded, forgetting that he was most likely watching the road. He apparently saw it, though, for he was responding promptly. 'Dee, are you sorry for last night? I know it hurt you a little bit, but honestly, love, it doesn't every time——'

'Oh, God!' she exploded, hiding all her pent-up uncertainties behind a sudden spurt of anger. 'Don't patronise me! I know I'm young, but I'm certainly not ignorant of the facts of life—they do teach things in school, you know!'. She stopped abruptly, felt his hand withdraw, and her voice changed. 'That's it, isn't it? You're regretting last night, not I. Is it because I'm so young? I believe it's called statutory rape when a legal adult has sex with a minor.' The words were staccato-swift and cutting as she struggled with her foolish desire not to cry.

'Stop it, just stop it!' Mike's voice rose over hers and she did, clamming up and staring away from him. 'All right, maybe I'm wondering if we did the right thing last night, what's wrong with that, for God's sake? For crying out loud, Dee, I'm twenty-nine years old—eleven years older than you. You aren't even eighteen!'

'And if I'd been forty?' she queried chillingly, and heard his impatient sigh. 'What then, answer me that? It wouldn't have mattered so much, would it, that you were eleven years younger than I was? You'd have considered yourself quite capable of dealing with it, wouldn't you? Wouldn't you?'

'That's ridiculous,' he gritted. His knuckles were white as his hands tightened spasmodically on the steering wheel.

'Why is it ridiculous?' she shouted, spilling all of her turbulent emotions out and sensing his wince. 'I knew what the hell I was doing, didn't I? What if I'd been a forty-year-old virgin? It still wouldn't have mattered so much—don't shake your head like that—it wouldn't! I can see it in your eyes. *Damn* it, you're looking at statistics again, and you aren't really seeing *me* under all that! When will it stop, Mike? When will people stop looking at me and saying "there's the millionaire heiress" or "there's the seventeen-year-old"! Do you know how I've been patronized at the restaurant, just because people think that if I'm a waitress I can't be that sharp in the brains department?'

'I can't overlook the facts, no matter how you may want me to!' he snapped, a host of thunderclouds lowering on his brow.

'I don't want you to! It's a fact that I was a virgin and I'm not now, and you're the one who took my virginity!' she hissed. 'And it's a fact that last night was something very special to me, and I think that if you'd let it, it would be special to you, too! And mister, it's a fact that you can either look at what we had last night as just having sex or making love. I don't want you to ignore the facts, man, I just want you to have the right perspective on them! Would you have minded so much if I hadn't been a virgin?'

Amazingly, a slight, quick smile quirked at his lips. 'I probably wouldn't be feeling so guilty,' he admitted ruefully.

'Well, then,' she said hardly, watching closely for his reaction, 'if I'd known, I would have lost my virginity in some raunchy little motel room with a total stranger, and then you wouldn't have to be feeling so bad.'

She was totally unprepared for his viciously bitten off oath, or the violent swerve of the car cutting off the highway and parking jerkily at the side of the road. He reached for her, grabbed her by the shoulders, and began to shake her hard. 'Don't you ever, ever say a thing like that again!' he snarled, and she wondered at his anger, even while a slow glow of warmth spread through her. 'My God! Don't you have any more respect for yourself than that? I've never——'

She stopped him simply by reaching forward and pressing her soft lips to his. Then she leaned back and smiled at him. 'And aren't you glad I had more respect for myself and you by making it much, much more special to me than just a tawdry one-night stand?' she asked him softly. 'Mike, do you really regret it? If so, I'm very sorry. I just can't.'

He relaxed his grip on her and sighed, replying, 'Maybe I think I should regret it. Maybe that's why I'm putting myself through such throes of guilt, I don't know. And yes, it was very, very special to me, and I'll treasure the memory.' He brought his lips down and caressed hers gently.

But she drew back and frowned into his shirt. 'Mike, why won't you tell me where we're going? Trust is one thing, but this is going a bit far, surely?'

He looked at her a moment. 'I've been putting it off,' he muttered, rubbing his eyes with his fingers. 'And you're right, I should have told you sooner. We're going to Knoxville.'

It was a flat statement, brooking no argument, and yet he paused, watching her closely. At his words, Dee felt a deep blow of dread in her chest, but she strove to overcome it, thinking to herself, trust. He wants me to trust him. Trust him, Dee. She drew a deep, shaky breath and asked, 'How long are we staying, then?' And for the life of her, she couldn't help looking the question *why?* at him, tensed. Why home, why now?

He relaxed slightly, smiled a little, and he cupped her cheek in that familiar way. 'You surpass all my expectations,' he told her quietly. 'We are, my girl, going to my apartment. We're going to test out that once-tried theory of yours and really see if the one place no one will look for you is at your own home base. My apartment is just downtown, not fifteen minutes from your house. And if my guess is right and if you manage to keep pretty much hidden, we should be able to limp along tolerably well for a while.'

Dee felt stunned, bewildered. 'But why? Why can't we go somewhere else for a while? Why do we have to go back home?' She stared at him, feeling that odd barrier from the morning, getting the strangest feeling that he wasn't telling her something, but she still couldn't pinpoint what it was. 'I don't understand.'

Mike straightened in his seat and stared out into the golden day. 'You said to me not too long ago that what you needed most was time to think, to decide what you were going to do. Have you made a decision?'

She hesitated, feeling swamped with uncertainty, puzzlement and the desire to tell him just how she really felt about him. But it was too new to her, too early for that, and she was silent a moment. Then, reluctantly, 'No, I haven't.'

His jaw hardened. 'Well, what I'm going to do is buy you that time you need.' Silence, and he muttered something under his breath, something quick and stern sounding, and very strange. Dee suspected that he hadn't really meant her to hear it, but she had very good hearing and she picked it up in spite of the softness with which it was spoken. 'I'm going to buy you all the time in the world.'

And she couldn't understand its gist, just as she couldn't understand the element of inexplicability to his behaviour, but since she had forced the issue so far, she didn't want to ask him anything else just yet.

He started the car again, pulled out into the barren stretch of highway and silence reigned for a long, long time in the confines of the car. And she sank back into her seat and puzzled at the many unexplained and unexplainable mysteries in her life.

They stopped soon to stretch their legs and to get a cold drink, and by then she had simply given up on her endless speculating and just concentrated on each moment. Life had begun to take on an element of unreality for her, for the events in the past four days had become too much to handle. Her emotions had been yanked all out of whack, and her whole schedule had been overturned, and now she had to reconstruct something new for herself. She was quite afraid, because she had settled into a comforting groove. She had known where she would be staying the next week, and she had begun to make plans and have hopes and dreams of the simple, every day sort: planning next week's menu according to her budget; the television specials she had looked forward to; whether she could afford that blue dress on display that she'd been eyeing for several days. Now she didn't know what to expect, or where she would next lay her head. It bewildered her so much that she had to simply shut down and cope with only non-essential, commonplace things.

It was strange, too, how she caught herself looking around for Mike and making sure that he was near. She'd never really done that before except when she had been a young child and had been too young to explore without her parents. She found that she was trying to reassure herself of his presence and support, and in a way this angered her, for she had become quite proud of her self-sufficiency early in life. She began to withdraw in little ways, and not in any particular way that he would especially notice, but he gradually stopped making general conversation as he sensed her silent mood.

Dee became increasingly grim as they neared the familiar, once-loved area she knew so well, the spring air of northern Ohio giving way to a more balmy warmth and greenery. She was conscious of Mike's flickered, questioning glances, but was in no mood to tell him of the strange feelings that were bombarding her. She felt that she was travelling further and further into a strange darkness that invaded her brain and hampered her thought processes. No matter where she turned her head, she saw darkness, in spite of the fact that the sun was benignly shining and the birds were blithely singing in chirrupy spurts. And the darkness that she saw and felt was an unreasoning dread. She was suddenly able to understand why her later memories of Kentucky were dark and misted over with a heavy veil. It was a cloud of remembered unhappiness.

She dozed fitfully, then she sank into a murky sleep that caught at her blood and forced it to slug slowly through her veins, and someone was really chasing her this time, and it wasn't Mike but an unknown menacing stranger, and she tried to run and run, but she was so hampered by her lifeless limbs that she couldn't get anywhere. 'I can't move,' she whimpered, and jerked with fright as she felt a warm hand descend on to her quaking shoulder, and she was caught, trapped, mired down in mud. She knew a terrible sinking feeling as she realised that she was caught for good. She would never get away or be free again . . . 'Trapped! I'm trapped!' she sobbed dryly, and was pulled into wakefulness by insistent hands.

Opening her eyes, she stared hugely up into Mike's concerned face. Then awareness and reality hit her and she straightened with a groan. They had pulled into a parking lot in the middle of an apartment complex, stylish, modern, and well maintained. Shoving a quick, slightly shaking hand through her hair, Dee muttered, not looking at Mike, 'Sorry. I was having a bad dream.' One hand left, but he rubbed at her collarbone with his other hand, thumb rotating gently.

'Are you sure you're all right?' His head was bent to her and he suddenly seemed too near, so she sat forward and found her shoes. She'd slipped them off earlier, and one was stuck under the car seat.

'I'm fine. It was a foolish dream, but then dreams always seem that way when you're awake and out of them.' She sent a slanting, wry glance up at him, a twisted smile on her lips. 'But when you're caught in them, they're as real as the edge of a knife that can slip and prick you if you aren't careful . . . I always thought that getting stuck in a nasty, sticky mud would be horrible, and I always dream of it, or getting caught and mired down some way. Filthy thought!'

Her shoes slipped on, she straightened and looked about her with interest, then sent a questioning gaze to the still figure beside her.

He smiled at her, easily, but the hand that had stayed

on her shoulder tightened as if he had felt the keen edge of the knife she had described. Then he was pointing out a group of windows that was his apartment, warning her that since he hadn't been back for a while, the place would be a mess.

Dee's mood lightened and she laughed at him as they struggled to get everything from the car into the building. He had been quite right: the place was a wreck, with an unlived-in air about the rooms and a layer of dust that was settled on the furniture not covered up, and a few boxes lying around, stacked to the brim with things that he swore he'd stored. She teased him unmercifully as they set about cleaning up the roomy place. The furniture was good, she discovered, and the few ornaments around were tasteful and both looked and felt expensive. She admired Mike's huge record collection as he dusted off cabinets, and peered at all his books with approval and interest. He had disappeared to the bedrooms to make them up and to check the kitchen and heating.

After tidying up the place, they set off to buy groceries, and in spite of Dee's voiceless apprehensions and darkening perspective, they had an uproarious time, skating a shopping cart dangerously through the aisles and making each other laugh helplessly. Dee ran into an older woman's cart and was treated with a hostile, disapproving stare, and Mike accidentally knocked over a stack of cereal boxes when she startled him by zooming around a corner unexpectedly.

Back at the apartment, they put away the food companionably, and she asked him curiously, 'Whatever are you going to do about Judith and Howard? You called them and told them you were coming back with me. What will happen when you don't show up with me, as promised?'

Mike bent and stuck his head into the refrigerator as he arranged the perishables neatly on the shelves. 'I called them later and told them that you'd gotten away, and that there would be a delay while I located you again.' The words echoed oddly in the small confines of the humming cubicle, and he backed out to shut it finally, only then glancing at her still body.

Dee asked quietly, feeling strange, 'When did you do that?'

He smiled at her cheerfully. 'When you were in the bathroom taking a shower this morning. It ought to give us both a lot of time to think, don't you agree? They're well aware of how slippery a fish you can be, when you choose to get away.'

She nodded, absently, her eyes vaguely puzzled, and the sudden descent of his hand on her bottom jerked her out of her thoughts with a small shriek. 'What was that for?' she exclaimed indignantly, trying in vain to slap him back.

He laughed down in her face. 'It was to get you started on my supper, slave,' he growled, and she made a rebellious face.

'I don't make suppers, or do windows, or clean bathrooms, or wash dishes . . .' she ticked off the items on her fingers, haughtily. Mike looked extremely indignant.

'And to think I spent all that money on a worthless slave! What in the world *do* you do?'

The peep she gave him from under her lashes was quite mischievously provocative. 'I could become quite a good massuese,' she replied, contemplatively, and he immediately appeared appeased.

'Well then, *that's* all right. But how are we going to live?'

She twinkled at him, 'T.V. dinners?' and had to laugh at his involuntary groan. Then she became brisk. 'No, no, I'll fix us something to eat, since you drove all day! Go on, get out, get out! Relax in the living room, for heaven's sake!' She shooed him out and he left, only

after giving her a laughing, tickling, hard kiss to which
she responded gladly.

She spent a busy hour in the kitchen, clanging pans
around cheerfully, having successfully shaken her dark
mood from earlier. She whisked around, setting the
table for two and washing up the dirty dishes as she
went, and eventually she went into the living room to
fetch Mike to the table. Walking softly on her toes in a
natural, athlete's walk that proclaimed her to the
knowledgeable as a sprinter, she moved swiftly into the
other room.

As she entered it, she slowed and stared through the
semi-darkness of the curtained room at the slumped
form on the couch, and stopped silently to stare at
Mike, concerned. He had his head in both hands, his
fingers tangled in what could only be an attitude of
grief, or sadness. Dee looked at his hands, remembering
fleetingly, with tenderness, how her hands had tangled
in his hair in almost the exact same way—was it only
this morning? 'Mike?' It came out soft. 'Are you okay?'

His head jerked up at her voice, and he was off of the
couch and walking her way, normal, casual. 'Of course.
I'm about ready to chew on the furniture, I'm so
hungry,' he teased, grinning at her.

She didn't return the smile, her eyes troubled. 'Are
you sure nothing's bothering you?' The change in him
was astounding; one moment he appeared to be
extremely depressed, and the next he was so completely
normal that she sensed even more strongly that
something was wrong.

'Not a blessed thing,' he said cheerfully, then he
rubbed at his eyes with thumb and forefinger. 'I think I
did too much driving lately, and my eyes are bothering
me, but other than that and the fact that I might die in
the next few minutes from starvation—why, I'm just
fine.'

Her eyes slowly crinkled at him and she had to

chuckle. 'All right, I get your drift! Come on, it's ready and waiting for you.'

Throughout that evening, as they watched television and played checkers, Mike was indeed so ordinary and calm, and quite cheerful, that she gradually began to believe that what she had seen earlier had been mostly her imagination. She enjoyed herself that evening, more than she had for a long time. He could make her laugh hysterically with his keen, dry wit and humorous, biting comments, and he could force her to concentrate more than anyone else could, driving her mind to quicker and keener decisions. He forced her to make snap decisions at the checker board, and she blundered terribly on the first game, flustered by his demands. But the second win came a bit harder for him, for she was beginning to meet his demands, and she had always been quick to react, intelligent and ready to trust her own judgment. And the third time, it was she who moved faster than he, goading him on when his long-fingered hand hesitated briefly over a certain play, and she flushed with triumph when she captured his final checker. 'Ha!' she jeered, wrinkling her nose and waving the last checker under his chagrined nose. 'You got it that time, my man! Didn't think I had it in me, did you?'

Her hand was captured easily, and his green eyes reached down deep into her as he smiled a lazy, heartstopping smile that touched her soul. 'I knew very well you had it in you, sweetheart,' he murmured, kissing her small hand quickly. It quivered. 'I'm the one who spent nine months learning just how much you do have in you, remember? And I think I'm only just beginning to dig beneath the surface. You shouted at me today, crying, "When are people going to stop putting labels on me!" and I didn't know how to respond, then. But you *are* all those things you listed, Dee, and not only those things but much, much more. And you've got to learn that people will see only what you show them—if you won't show them what's underneath, then they'll never know the special part that's the essence of you.'

Unexpected tears pricked her eyes. How had they got so serious, so suddenly? Her eyes slid away from his and her nose and throat stopped with the tears she was trying hard not to shed. 'But how?' she whispered, and caught at herself before going on. 'How do you take the hurt and the cruelty?' Her hand twisted in his. 'How do you take the indifference?'

Mike stroked her hand into quietness. 'My poor, sweet girl—is that how you see life? Really? Or is that what you've been taught, in the past few years? You ran away from the unhappiness at home physically, but you took it with you as you ran, didn't you? You kept the memory alive, and you were determined to keep that from ever happening again, so you walled yourself into a busy little life and an empty little hole of an apartment. You weren't going to be pushed away by anyone else, ever again, because you were going to make sure that no one got that close. You really were on the run, all the time you were settled in one place, and you'd be on the run now, if you hadn't smashed right into me.'

Shaken, Dee averted her head as her face crumpled into misery. 'Don't, please,' she muttered, tugging uselessly at her hand. Mike began to pull her towards him, though, inexorably, and she finally just collapsed into the warm circle he offered her. A sob shook her, and then another. She buried her face as she recognised the soul-shaking truth of what he had said to her, and she whispered, mouth trembling, 'I just don't want to be hurt any more.'

'God!' The word was wrenched from him, right out from the deepness of his chest, from his awareness, and it sounded anguished somehow, sad and tortured. His arms tightened convulsively on her, and she welcomed it, both the pain and the comfort, for they were both the same. His face went to her hair and she felt the jutting bone of his cheek, the press of his browbone, and the moving sensation of his lips. Then he was bending, picking her up, carrying her into the other room. It all happened so fast that her breath felt torn away from the wonderful emotional shock of the unexpected. In the darkness of the bedroom, he put her down and wordlessly undressed her with an urgency that left her shaking. Then she was helping him undress and they were loving each other, warm and intense and so giving that she didn't know where to put all the love and emotion. It spilled over on to the sheets with her dripping tears as she was overcome with the need and the feel and the love of him.

Much later, he was holding her very, very tightly and tenderly, wrapping his arms around her with a firmness and a tight demand that kept her right up to the vitality of his damp, hot, exhausted body. Silence smoothed over the darkness in a wash of tranquillity, and she jumped with the unexpectedness of his voice, oddly compelling. 'Dee—Deirdre. Promise me something, sweetheart, please. Can you bring yourself to promise me this one thing?'

She smiled into his skin and lifted her head slightly to try and stare into his face. It was a pale-hewn sketch of his features, drawn in blacks and greys. 'You know I'd promise you anything,' she said quietly, and felt the impact of her words slice through him.

'I don't deserve to ask this of you, I shouldn't say anything at all,' he muttered, tracing her cheek with one hand, going over and over it as if he would like to imprint the feel and the texture of her for ever in his mind. 'Sweet heaven, I shouldn't be saying this, but—I can't help it. Oh, Dee, you have no idea of what I'm talking about. But you've just got to believe in the humanity and goodness of man and never, ever doubt it. Damn, you don't understand me, and I can't explain, but—oh, please, Dee, just have faith in mankind, just have faith!'

And she thought she had never experienced such an intense and fulfilling happiness, even as she wondered blankly what he had meant.

The next morning she woke slowly, leisurely, luxuriously, and stretched like a satisfied and happy cat, muscle by muscle, glorying in her own inherent sexuality in a way she had never before. She was a woman, in every sense of the word, and she loved being a woman. Her head turned and her hand went over the sheets, encountering nothing but pillow and blanket. Mike was gone. He was probably fixing breakfast, she surmised, running her eyes slowly over the contents of the room. She liked it. It was plain and yet comfortable, and it somehow embodied the flavour of him. She savoured it. Perhaps it was his scent that lingered on the pillow next to hers, or perhaps it was the casual indications of his presence in the carelessly laid comb and brush, and the cufflinks that were glittering like goldfish in a shallow bowl. She definitely liked his masculine presence in her life. She liked it very much indeed.

After a few lazy yawns, she slid out of bed and made it quickly and neatly. Then she padded to the small bathroom that belonged exclusively to the master bedroom, then showered and washed her hair as fast as she could, impatient with the small delay in starting her day. After towelling dry and dressing, she ran Mike's comb through her curls so they would not dry all snarled, then she bounded down the hall, eager to give him a special good morning kiss.

It was strange that she felt no insecurities about Mike and the future. She sensed something in him that seemed to speak to the emotion in her. Can one accurately sense something like that? she wondered idly.

Could that kind of sensitivity be trusted? She wondered
what would happen if she were in a crowd of people
with him, or a full room. Would she be able to sense his
presence and direction of thought then, or was it all an
illusion . . .

The sound of voices hit her a split second before the
impetus of her moving body carried her into the living
room, and she was so totally unprepared for the blow
of intense shock that struck her that it was as if
someone had physically hit her, and hard.

'. . . you really were very, very clever, weren't you,
Mr Carradine?' And that voice was one she knew. It
was the voice of her aunt Judith. And Dee couldn't stop
her entrance into the room, for the messsage to move
had already been sent to her muscles and was being
obeyed, even while the shock of discovery was slammed
into her midriff, like a knife. Judith was still talking and
she was hearing the words, though she wanted for all
the world to stop her ears and block them out for ever.
'How in the world did you trick her into coming to
Knoxville, of all places, without giving your hand
away?'

Then she was in the room, just barely inside the
room, and she was trapped utterly and completely. It
was the nightmare that was reality, and the darkness
swamped her, eating at her soul. Her mind screamed at
the horror, as she took in the scene of Judith standing
near to Mike, who was facing the window looking
outside, his back ramrod-stiff, straight. Dee noticed
with a fleeting irrelevance that his hair was sleekly,
neatly brushed and that he was dressed in a tailored
black suit with a crisp white shirt. It suited him. Then
her eyes, wide and uncomprehending, slewed to the
shorter, squatter figure of her aunt, who had turned at
her entrance and was watching her with a secretive,
triumphant smile on her plump face. It was a very nasty
smile. Howard, she noticed, almost as an afterthought,

was slumped in an easy chair in the habitual cringing attitude he constantly adopted, as if life were too much for him to bear, or Judith. The still, straight figure at the window did not move. He could have been an unliving statue.

After the first wide-eyed, incredulous, uncomprehending stare, Dee's face assumed a semblance of normality, though she did not come right into the room. It was all surface; inside, she felt the plunge of the knife sink to her life's centre and the burning tip of the painful hot steel of despair started a slow turning.

Trust, she thought, a last desperate chance to believe that he hadn't meant it, hadn't counted on this happening. It was all a huge, monstrous mistake, a colossal error in logic, an underestimation of the opposition. Judith and Howard had obviously had his apartment watched. That was it, surely that was it.

But then Judith was dispelling that last illusion with a cruel accuracy, hitting her thoughts by an accident of chance. 'He was very good, dear, wasn't he?' she asked, a sly maliciousness in her smile, if not in her voice. Her voice was all cooing affection and falsity. 'We never lost faith in him . . .' and Dee flinched violently at her ironic choice of words, '. . . all those months. We knew he would bring you back to us, dear girl. Of course, he had an excellent incentive, didn't he? But he wouldn't have told you about the staggering bonus we offered him for your return. And it was all well earned. Well earned, indeed! Well, girl, have you got your things packed in your suitcase? We've got quite a lot to do today, and we haven't much time to wait for you. Your room, of course, is ready and waiting for you.' Her light, almost colourless eyes watched Dee avidly, storing up all her expressions and watching for any sign of betraying vulnerability.

But Dee wasn't even paying attention to her aunt, for she was watching that straight, stiff back. Walking slowly across the room, right by Judith without so much as a sidelong glance, she halted just behind Mike, right close to his shoulder. She could have moved slightly and touched him, she was so close. But she didn't. Then, with a quick, stern glance behind her shoulder at the nearby, hovering woman, she said with dignity, 'This is private, if you don't mind.' And at that, Judith, out of a social courtesy, had to withdraw to the other side of the room. Then, facing that quiet figure that stared out of the window and feeling as if she were about to scream from the horrible pain of the knife, Dee whispered shakingly. 'Mike—oh, Mike! I don't believe them. You couldn't do this. They had your apartment watched, didn't they? You didn't—tell them, did you?' Trust, she thought, tasting bitter ashes in her mouth. She was asking for his side of the story, but she didn't believe that last plea of hers. It was the death throes of her trust speaking.

'Yes, I did.' The words were a whisper, like hers, and the knife twisted in deeper. She put a hand to his shoulder, and it felt warm and vital, living rock. He didn't even flinch or turn around. She could see the clean line of his jaw and the dark curl of his eyelashes as he stared unblinkingly out of the window. She got the strangest impression that he was not seeing what he was staring at.

'God!' It was a wounded cry, no matter how low she whispered it. Though he didn't move, she saw a muscle in his jaw jerk spasmodically. 'You said have faith! You said to me, last night, to have faith! How can I have faith when everyone around me is so damnably faithless?'

'I said have faith in humanity, Dee.' And he turned at that, glanced at her emotionlessly, the look in his eyes completely blank. 'Not in me.'

Something died, right there in front of her, on the carpet, bleeding. She stared at it, head down for a few minutes, and when she looked up that something dead was in her eyes and it was a terrible sight. Mike stared at her and then turned back to the window, an automaton. 'Can you,' she whispered dully, wondering why she was twisting the knife in further and wondering why there was no more pain, 'look me in the eyes and tell me that you don't want me here?' Silence, and he tensed. She could feel it with every nerve of her body, every fibre of her soul.

CHAPTER EIGHT

BUT then she laughed, and that too was a terrible sound. 'Never mind,' she said. 'Because do you know what? I don't believe in humanity any more.' She turned very slowly because if she didn't she would fall down and not get up, ever. And then with measured paces, she walked carefully to the door. Don't feel, don't feel—ah, Mike don't! Her thoughts screamed and screamed, and she wondered when they would ever stop screaming. She didn't even know why; everything else inside her felt so dead she might never feel again, and that was a blessing. The nightmare was real, but the reality was a nightmare and she should be waking soon. It was time to wake up. It was time to snap out of the dream, but she couldn't, because she knew she was pretending, to make things easier. As she reached the hall she heard Mike speak, and the words he was saying were so incredible, so horribly, utterly terrible that she jerked to a stop and turned again, face dead white, hands clenched tightly, and her whole slim body so tense that she thought something would crack.

'Mrs Kimble,' he said deeply, turning away from the window and being silhouetted against the bright sun's glare, 'the little matter of the bonus is something we need to discuss. You see, I know about the plot to kill Dee. Two failings in as many days is a rather rotten efficiency, don't you think? It was just a little too much to believe, just a bit too obvious. You should have told me from the beginning, Mrs Kimble. I could have helped you with the details. But now—well, it's a different matter. Everything's totally different. I know now, and I'm feeling a bit left out, not being included in the plans. It may just cost you a little more because of that, Mrs Kimble.'

The world stopped, just stopped stock still. Then it tilted so sickeningly and Dee felt her balance go, starting to topple forward. The silhouette at the window moved so quickly he was a blur, and he caught her before she hit the floor. But she wasn't unconscious, because life was too cruel to let her faint. When she felt those wonderfully familiar and yet horrifyingly unfamiliar arms close around her, she screamed and fought him so violently and with such a single-mindedness that he had to let go of her before she hurt herself.

She fell to the ground like a wounded animal, thinking to herself hazily, and I thought there could be no more pain. They won't have to kill me. I'm already dying.

'Clever, clever man,' Judith was saying admiringly, and the admiration was cold. 'So those bungling fools really did let the cat out of the bag, did they? When did you figure it all out?'

'After the first time. It didn't take me long,' he spoke, moving back to the window. Howard slumped further in his chair. A bird sang piercingly just outside the window. Dust motes danced in the sunlight. Dee managed somehow to drag herself to a chair and to pull herself into it. She might not have been there, as much attention as everyone was giving her. She might already be dead for all they noticed.

Always being overlooked, ignored, always being lonely. God, what a memory, she thought calmly. She'd done a good job of escaping—she really had. Nine months before he found her. She might even try again, if they were careless with watching her. But it didn't really matter now, because no matter how she would try, she would never escape again. The prison was inside her now. She would never be able to trust, to let herself love again. She didn't really care if she lived or died, and really would prefer to be dead. That joy of living that she had gone off to seek, those months ago, had finally been destroyed by the enemy.

'So you're wanting a little extra . . .' Judith mused, turning and walking slowly across the room. 'A little extra to keep your mouth shut, or a little extra to enlist your aid in our task? No, I think if we're to be sure you keep quiet, we'll have to expect you to help with the execution of the plan. Then you would be an accomplice and as guilty as the rest of us.' She glanced sharply at him. 'Could you do that, Mr Carridine? Could you help us?'

'Whatever it takes,' he said steadily. Dee heard him and didn't seem to react at all. The room was getting a little fuzzy around the edges. Wasn't it rich to have her lover plotting to kill her? Wasn't it just absolutely rich? The room snapped back into a sharper clarity than it had ever been before. She straightened in her chair and her blue eyes sharpened into a hard brightness, her mind ticking swiftly over. Rich, but not as rich as she would have been in a month and a half. If Mike was as mercenary as all that, why hadn't he taken the smart way out and stuck with her, the original heiress, the one in a position to ultimately give him the most?

Foolish, foolish . . . her eyes swung to his silhouette and he seemed to be looking at her. If his reasons for giving her away to her guardians were not mercenary reasons—and the very fact that he had apparently betrayed her and thus lost her confidence and trust would prove that he was not mercenary—then that would mean that his reasons were something else entirely.

Everyone was talking over her and around her, terms being discussed, plans being made, macabre, terrible plans, but she wasn't even listening. She was sitting there quite calmly, her face no longer that terrible shade of white, thinking. She was totally unaware of the fact that she was being watched quite closely by that silhouette by the window. If he had a reason, then she could find it sooner or later. She was coming out of the shock and was no longer willing to take things at face value. And something was not quite right.

She didn't even feel any shock at the ease with which she was able to accept that her guardians wanted her dead. Retrospect guided her right along the path that Mike had taken and she saw his reasoning, realising it was sound. She was the only thing that stood between her aunt and millions of dollars. Dee, the daughter of a sister she had begun to hate and resent. Dee, the pretty girl she should have had but couldn't, just as Dee's father was the wealthy man she should have married but didn't. It was all so glaringly obvious that she marvelled at her own stupidity at having never seen it before. Or hadn't she? Hadn't she run away when things became too much? Was that because she had sensed the antipathy in the house, and her own instinct for survival had prompted her to bolt from home? She'd exclaimed to Mike not so very long ago that this life had been killing her. Perhaps her subconscious had sensed that it had been more than just a figure of speech.

And Mike was going to buy her all the time in the world. Her eyes narrowed on Judith, cat-like, looking extremely calculating, and everything fell into place. She knew what Mike was up to now. 'You are such a fool, Judith,' she heard herself say, crystal clearly. 'Such an utter fool.'

The other woman swung around and stared at her with such a wealth of malevolence and antipathy gleaming in her small eyes that Dee had to swallow, taken aback at the sight of so much unreasoning, active hate.

'It appears to me, miss,' Judith hissed, coming

forward and looking as if she'd dearly love to strike her, 'that you're not in any position to be saying much of anything at the moment, so I'd keep damn well quiet, if I were you!'

'It does appear that way,' Dee replied calmly, and saw the figure at the window move at last. 'But I don't believe I shall remain silent, all the same. I—I just don't understand you. I don't understand you! Why do you hate me so? Why are you doing this? There's enough money, more than enough for all of us! Don't you realise that if you'd just once shown me a bit of true kindness, I would have been more than happy to share everything I have with you? My God, don't you know that if—if you'd only given me a little love instead of this terrible, senseless animosity, I would have given you the world . . .' Unwanted and useless tears pricked her eyes and she brushed her face impatiently. She shouldn't, not for them. They weren't worth it. They weren't worth—a drop of wetness splashed on her hands, then another.

She was shocked at Judith's harsh, mocking laughter, a sound that reverberated through her whole being and haunted her for quite some time afterwards. 'Why do you suppose we'd think you worth the effort?' the older woman sneered, stalking close to eye her up and down with a loathing that was all too apparent. 'And why do you think we'd be content with the crumbs that you'd see fit to throw our way when we could have it all! Oh, it's so easy! It's so incredibly easy! Don't you know that I could crush you like an ant with one careless finger and never mourn the loss? Alice was a fool, but then she always was a fool! She actually expected me to be happy caring for her child, ready to accept the burden of someone who stood between me and everything I've always dreamed of! It was a stupid mockery, that pittance—' and the word was a poisonous spat of hate and envy and destroying greed, '—of an allowance. An insult to me! A damned slap in the face!'

'It wasn't!' Dee screamed, out of hurting for the memory of a mother so loved and needed and yearned for, and a mother so irrevocably gone. 'It wasn't! You could have had more than enough money put away, if you'd only saved your allowance while you lived at the house and had all your expenses paid! *What does the money matter?* I don't understand!' Her total incomprehension made the statement a cry of bewilderment and remembered pain. 'It brings me more grief and trouble than anything I know. I hate it, do you hear me—*hate* it!'

'Well then, isn't that convenient!' Judith retorted, pacing around Dee's chair in a predatory manner that had her shrinking down into her seat. 'Because you aren't going to get it! All my life I've stood by and watched Alice get it all—all of it! Everything!' Her hand flew out in convulsive, blinded anger and out of the corner of her eye Dee saw Howard shrink away as if Judith had hit him. 'She had youth! She had beauty, and a damnable charm that I could never imitate, no matter how I tried! And in the end she had dear, handsome Charles, and so much money she could have shared more with me, a whole fortune more and—my God!—never would have even missed it! While Howard here,' she swept out a contemptuous hand and he cringed away even more, 'hadn't enough sense to hold down a decent job for more than a few months or a year at a time! And in the end, dear, lovely Alice got hers. Oh yes, in the end all of her youth and beauty and wealth got her nowhere, nowhere!'

Dee couldn't stop the deluge of grief that shook her at the callous dismissal of the bright and beloved personality that had once meant the entire world to her. 'Her own sister! Oh God, her own sister——'

She heard the other woman say abruptly, 'Well then,

:hat's it. It's a shame that those men we hired were
fools, otherwise it'd be over now. But Carridine will
help us, and that's a surprise, Howard, isn't it? We'd
had him figured differently, but he's just another Judas,
like everyone else in the world.' She cocked her head in
a grotesque caraciture of a bright bird and eyed Dee
with a contemplative look that was utterly repulsive.
'Suicide, perhaps. A slashing of the wrists would be
messy, but effective. We could put her in the bathroom
in her room, to avoid too much of a mess. Or there's
strangulation. You could hang yourself, but where
would we put you?'

Horrified disgust swamped Dee and she burst out
uncontrollably, 'My God, how can you stand there and
tell me so calmly that you are—are actually able to
contemplate—which one of you would cut my wrists?
What kind of an animal are you?'

'A crazed one,' a calm, deep voice intervened at last,
like a breath of sanity in the terrible confrontation.
Everyone turned as one to look at the man who had
spoken. He was lounging against the wall near the
window, hands in pockets, looking lazy, his green,
green eyes surveying everything alertly. 'An outcast of
humanity. A maverick. A manifestation of evil, if you
like. There are many, many descriptions for things like
her.' The words literally dripped his utter distaste and
contempt. He looked at Dee and slowly smiled into her
eyes. 'And so you figured it out, just like I'd known you
would. I saw the very instant when it all occurred to
you. It happened quicker than I'd thought it would,
darling. You can come into the room now, Darrell.'
And at these strange words, a youngish, blond man
who was powerfully built walked into the room from
the hall. He had come out of the spare bedroom.

Howard and Judith were identical pictures of
incredulity and shock. Their eyes fairly popped out of
their heads at this unexpected development. Apparently

they could handle blackmail and plotting a death more easily than discovery.

Mike said to Dee, 'I'd like for you to meet a friend and colleague of mine, Darrell Krause. We went to school together some time back. I called him this morning before calling your guardians, and we set up a few bugs while you were so peacefully slumbering.' He turned to the astounded and dismayed Kimbles. 'We've been recording everything that's been said today. We have your admissions of guilt on tape. There's absolutely no way to extricate yourselves from this.'

Dee had nodded her head at his words, unsurprised, and she stood rather aimlessly and rubbed tiredly at her forehead. Then she looked around her with a blank expression and said quietly, 'This isn't happening. Life isn't this bizarre, it really isn't. People wanting to kill me, private investigators popping out of the woodwork—insanity, that's what it is! I've gone mad.' The world seemed to be fuzzed over in an unfocussed way, as if there was a layer of cotton wool between her and everyone else. It was a rather nice insulation; shock, she thought irrelevantly, can be quite soothing. Your system shuts down until you have the strength to let everything sink in.

She heard footsteps come her way and Mike was asking her, concerned, 'Dee, are you all right?'

She heard him, turned her head and would have answered, except that just at that moment there was a blur of movement from her left and she was looking on reflex to see what it was. Her eyes slewed that way just in time to see Judith reach swiftly into the pocket of her light suit jacket and pull out something remarkably wicked-looking, for as small as it was. Dee's gaze went to it and finally her mind grasped what it was. It was a gun.

That insulation of cotton wool was not entirely beneficial, she thought dazedly, as she stared into the face of that small black death and found she couldn't move. It was just like that mire of mud that she always dreamt about, holding her in place, trapping her for ever, and she was going to die any second now as Judith snarled out something that she didn't quite catch. She could tell that it was full of her unreasoning hate and rage, though, and then the gun was lifted to be aimed right at her.

She had just enough time to think, I really am going to get it this time, and then everything exploded around her. Something catapulted into her right side and it knocked her all the way over to the wall, which she hit with such a hard thud that she coughed in pain and protest. As she was pushed roughly to the side, she heard a sharp report and felt an angry buzzing sting at her cheek, as if a wasp had got her. Then she saw the blond man named Darrell hurtle himself like a football player right into the dumpy figure of Judith and they both went down like a load of bricks, Judith underneath and howling in pain and anger. Howard took off like a rabbit for the door but was stopped when Mike gathered himself into a crouch at her feet and shot off like a guided missile, cannoning into Howard's back much in the same way that Darrell had smashed into Judith.

Howard staggered but didn't fall, and he turned to aim a wild blow at Mike which Dee, sitting on the floor and watching the whole scene like television, could have told him wouldn't do any good. Mike was quicker than sight, ducking and simply no longer there by the time Howard's relatively slow fist had reached the place where he'd been. It was almost like watching someone in slow motion, that was how much faster Mike was than he, and Howard was suddenly lying on the carpet and holding a hand to his profusely bleeding nose and mouth. Mike shook his hand as if it hurt him, and he turned to see what was happening to Darrell and

Judith. Dee's head, in imitation, swung to the left like a
pendulum and she saw Darrell get up from sprawling
all over her aunt, that black gun in his capable-looking
hand. He rubbed one cheek where he looked to be
scratched. Judith was panting on the floor, greying hair
all askew, and eyes so full of a molten animalistic fury
and spitting hate that Dee was quite happy to be sitting
where she was on the floor, quite out of range.

Then there came such a stream of vile filth from
Judith's mouth that Mike turned to her wearily and
said shortly, 'Shut up, before I shut you up.' He didn't
raise his voice, but her words were suddenly cut off as if
a door had been closed.

Dee just sat like a small child on the floor by the
bookcase she'd been shoved into, with fallen books all
around her and fair hair tousled from the unexpected
way she had been thrown about. Her hand went to her
cheek in reflex as the stinging didn't go away, and when
she felt something sticky, she brought it away and
looked at the red on her fingers. The bullet sent her way
must have winged her slightly.

Darrell asked, 'Is everyone all right?' and looked her
way along with Mike and, incidentally, Howard and
Judith. She heard an exclamation and Mike started for
her, but what she mostly heard was Judith.

'Pity,' the other woman said maliciously, 'I hadn't
meant to miss.' Then Mike was right beside her, putting
a gentle arm around her and reaching into his pocket
with the other free hand, extracting a white handkerchief
which he pressed carefully to her cheek, blotting the
blood flow. He pulled back the handkerchief and
inspected her cheek.

'It isn't bad at all,' he told her, gently reassuring.
'It's only about an inch long, and it should stop
bleeding in a minute or two. Here, take this and press
it to the cut and I'll go and get the first aid kit.' Dee
obediently took the soiled handkerchief and kept it in

place while he disappeared. As Mike then applied stinging antiseptic to her sore cheek and placed a band-aid against the small wound, Judith and Howard picked themselves up, while Howard mopped up his face as best he could. No one really seemed to notice him much, or care if he bled all over himself like a pig. But then, Dee mused, Howard always had been overlooked. It was the story of his life.

She found to her dismay that her cotton protection was beginning to wither away, and reaction was setting in. She crept over to the curtains and pulled them open the rest of the way. The others were talking and Mike and Darrell seemed to be making plans, but she wasn't paying attention. She was busy trying to understand just why she was feeling so utterly lonely, so terribly shaken up, when the only thing that had happened was what could have been expected. She could handle it. She wasn't the type to have hysterics. Still, she thought, her mouth shaking as she stared fixedly out the window, it wasn't every day that one gets shot at and nearly killed, and I've nearly died three times in as many days. It's enough to get anyone upset.

But what she found herself trying to cope with, and failing miserably, was how Mike had omitted to tell her of his plans. He had not only placed her in a position of severe jeopardy, but he had manipulated her with a fine arrogance, not even respecting her enough to tell her. It made her so very angry she wasn't sure what she would do if he came too close, too soon. She wasn't in control, she found, as she gripped the heavy curtains, white-knuckled, at her side.

Then she heard footsteps come up behind her, and knew who it was going to be. She knew quite well who those footsteps belonged to, and he was coming too close, too soon, for she didn't have her anger leashed yet. It was like a crouching animal, unfettered, ready to strike. Watch out, she thought, don't touch me or I'll

blow up right in your face. I'm too furious, just too
outraged at what you did to me . . .

. . . And his hand came down gently on to her
shoulder, just as she'd known it would, massaging the
rigidity of her neck muscles, and the white-hot fury in
her exploded, just as she'd known it would. For the
second time in less than a week she swung around, hand
tight in a fist, and totally without remorse hit him as
hard as she could in the jaw. And as he staggered back
that one step for balance, she was off and running for
the door and shooting out into the hall faster than she
had ever moved in her life.

CHAPTER NINE

DARRELL leaned casually against the couch and surveyed Judith and Howard sitting in two chairs, the gun propped in one hand. He said mildly, 'See? I told you she'd be sore.'

Mike looked at him, white and stern, and said harshly, 'Shut up, will you?' He shot for the door, calling over his shoulder, completely unaware of the contradiction in his commands, 'And get busy and call the police, too!'

Dee was already outside and moving fast. She cut through a few apartment buildings and angled back for the road. There were just too many places for her to go in that building complex. She had the advantage over Mike, as she pelted through the buildings and started running down the street. She could lose him.

She did. In a short space of time she was quite a distance away, jogging steadily, and the physical exertion eased away some of the excess of emotion that had been bottled up inside of her. It was good just to be on the move, to have that illusion of freedom and to pretend that she was carefree. The clean air stirred her cheek and the sun beat down on her head with a life-giving warmth. Eventually, walking and running at intervals, she found herself outside the city zoo, and realised she had gone several miles. She stood, breathing hard and looking up at the sign that was near the gateway, seeing the free admission for the day. Then moving more slowly as she caught her breath, she went on through the gates.

She walked around, feeling the tightness around her chest and heart ease, and pretended to look at the animals with everyone else. A small boy ran into her legs and she grabbed him before he fell, sending him laughingly back to his apologetic mother. Then, spying an empty bench along the well-kept walkway, she went and sat down to bask in the sunshine.

She was just killing time and she knew it. If she really wanted to she supposed she could run off right now and survive, even though she had no money. But it wouldn't serve any purpose now. The great escape had been a fine adventure and an excellent way to keep hold of her sanity, but there were just some things she couldn't run from. They had had quite a few shared experiences, she and Mike. Some of it had been really rotten, and some of it very frightening, but a lot had been good. They both had been thrown into abnormal circumstances, though. She knew that she would love Mike probably for the rest of her life, no matter what happened, but she was also reasonable enough to acknowledge that they had some very steep obstacles ahead of them, if they were both willing to work for a future in their relationship. One of her fears was that she wasn't sure if he was even willing to continue to see her.

There was the problem of their age difference. She personally didn't have a problem with it, but she knew that he felt a bit strange being involved with someone as young as she, and she couldn't guarantee that problems wouldn't arise from her extreme youth. She still had college to finish. How would he feel if she wanted to move to a different city for scholastic reasons, when he had his ties here?

There was also the huge problem of what she was going to do with all her money. That, she ruefully acknowledged, was going to be the hardest problem of all. She could potentially buy and sell a dozen private investigators. Mike had pride. It would gall him, she knew, to be supported by so much money. He would want to support her, himself. He would never be sure if she would resent him for forcing her to make a choice between the way of life that she could afford and his life. It would probably destroy them.

Damn that money! Dee beat the bench with one clenched fist and then winced. It was always getting in the way of her happiness, always causing more problems than it was worth. She had never asked to be rich: she would be more than happy to be just as ordinary as anyone else, working for a living, feeling pride in what she did. If only—her eyes narrowed against the sun. If only.

The afternoon was beginning to slide away when a tall shadow fell across her bent head. She looked up, saw him standing silently there, and checked her watch. 'You're slipping,' she said calmly. 'I expected to see you about an hour and a half ago.'

He didn't look very calm standing there, his hands clenched tensely, his face white, his eyes vivid with some kind of leaping emotion. 'I haven't been thinking very logically today,' he said quietly, and came to sit beside her. Turning her head to look at him with that same deep calm, Dee caught sight of the mark on his jaw.

'I was sorry the first time I hit you,' she remarked. 'I wasn't sorry today. I meant it.'

He just looked at her. It was a very hurting kind of look and yet accepting. 'I know. I deserved it.'

Damn her eyes—she couldn't see him suddenly. She turned her face away but not before he saw. She heard the catch in his breath. 'Yes, you did. You know, I guess we just have different views of friendship and trust, that's all. It means something different to you than it does to me.'

'Don't,' he whispered. 'Please don't. It wasn't meant to be like that. Really it wasn't.'

'It was!' She caught herself up and then went on. 'It was. You didn't trust me to be able to handle the situation, so you were going to just thrust me into it, all unaware of what was going on, because you thought that it would protect me, didn't you? You thought that if I didn't know what was going on I would be able to react in a more convincing manner than if I'd just been faking it. You were going to play out the big, omniscient hero scene, just another damned ego trip!'

'That's not entirely true, Dee,' he said softly, and it was the same as when he'd interrupted Judith's tirade. He didn't even have to raise his voice. Something in his tone and in his manner made her stop more effectively than if he'd shouted an order. 'You aren't seeing the whole picture clearly. You're only guessing at my reasons, and though you're very good, you haven't got the whole of it yet. Let me explain.'

Her throat was strangely stopped up and she cleared it, found she still couldn't say anything without the risk of breaking into those easy tears, so she nodded jerkily.

Mike hesitated. 'I somehow realised the danger that I'd brought you, very soon after that first attempt on your life, and I can't take any credit for rationally thinking it out. It was an intuitive leap, a fluke if you will. You told me at lunch a few days ago how your home was no longer the welcome and familiar place it had been, and you mentioned casually that your aunt had gotten rid of all the old family staff, gradually replacing them with the ones she'd picked personally. It wasn't much, but I had heard of a similar case of that happening, only the person who had fired the servants had been the son of a wealthy man who was trying to disorientate his ailing, elderly father in order to have him committed. The poor fellow had been going senile anyway, and it was fairly easy to get him institutionalised. So, your story sounded familiar to me, and out of a sudden impulse I asked you who would inherit the money at your death. Remember?'

'Oh yes.' Dee looked back and she could remember his strange, shocked look, the sudden stillness, the odd seriousness. 'You acted rather odd at the time, but I'd thought it was just a mood.'

'They must have been planning this for quite some time. A few days ago it wasn't much, and I wasn't sure, but it was enough to scare me half to death,' said Mike conversationally, and the content of his words was at such odds with the normality of his tone that Dee looked at him sharply. He was not casual, as his tone had suggested; the whiteness around his clenched hands and the area around his mouth betrayed that much to her. 'And then they tried to kill you a second time. You see, it was my fault that they'd been able to get to you in the first place. I led them right to you, right smack to you, and I would have been responsible for your death if you'd been killed, just as much as they.'

'No!' she protested, horrified at the extent to which he was taking his guilt. 'You couldn't have been responsible. You didn't know!'

'I suspected!' he ground out, self-accusation running rife through every fibre of him. 'I suspected and I allowed myself to be duped into a false sense of security! I told myself that it was too preposterous, too far-fetched, that I was making too much out of a random occurrence! I told myself that those two had been drunk and ready for mischief that night. I slipped up, Dee! I should have gone to the back with you in that laundrymat to check out the place. It's standard procedure, and I didn't do it. And I realised that I should have gone back there just that split second too late. To top it all off, when you screamed I ran to the back like an untried rookie. I know better than that! You never run into an unknown situation without taking precautions, but when I heard you scream, everything I'd been taught went right out of my head. All I could think of was that you were being hurt and frightened—if you'd died that day, it would have been my fault.'

Dee shot out a hand and gripped his tightly, shaking it. 'No! It wouldn't have been your fault, because you're human and you make errors just like everyone else! And that isn't even an error in judgment. That was just a simple weighing of the facts, and the facts that you had available to you just weren't enough to base a solid opinion on. You said yourself that you made an intuitive leap and not a rational one—you suspected, but you weren't to know, not really! Stop blaming yourself for something that didn't even happen. I didn't die, and it's thanks to you that I'm alive today.'

'You could have very easily died, and I led them right to you,' he insisted stubbornly, though his hand turned under hers to grip her tightly. She sighed with impatience.

'You weren't to know that, for heaven's sake! You were just doing a routine search for a runaway. How were you to know that they were just using you to find me in order to have me killed? That's ridiculous, Mike, and you know it.' There was no reply to that and she waited, finally saying, 'Are you going to tell me the rest of your story?'

'Are you sure you want to hear it?' he countered, then sighed. 'Sorry—of course you do. Anyway, I realised what was going on at that second attempt on your life—God, that was a nightmare, driving around in circles, looking for you and going crazy. I knew that we had no evidence to convict your guardians with and that you wouldn't be safe until I could pinpoint them specifically for attempted murder. I also knew that it wouldn't be long before that quick mind of yours put everything together for yourself, and I think I know what your reaction would have been. You'd have run away from it, believing you could keep safe that way. I hated to think of what could have happened to you. They wouldn't have given up, you know. They would have kept searching for you and I—hated to see you harassed like that. I'd begun to realise just how I'd hounded you, myself. You had the right to your privacy and independence, no matter what your age. I'd started to care for you very much, you see. You were no longer just a teenage runaway who might not have enough sense or wits to take care of you. God, I should be the first to admit just how much wit you really have—you certainly led me on a merry chase! I'll never have an inflated opinion of my skills as a private investigator again!' He laughed suddenly, wryly, mouth twisted in self-mockery.

Dee had to smile at that. 'What is it?'

The look he sent her was enough to send her chuckling. It was roguish and rueful, and somehow rakish too, with those brilliant, dancing eyes—how she loved those eyes! 'I was so sure I'd have you back home, repentant and safe within the first month. It was the only reason I took the job. Then I got piqued, and then I got so intrigued by the ingenious and inventive stunts you pulled that I was hooked! It wasn't just a matter of professional pride that kept me after you—I had an insatiable curiosity to know what you were really like. Every new clue was like the unveiling of a new and complex personality, challenging, stimulating, exciting. I was intellectually taken with you, and after a while I was emotionally taken with you. I wanted to see you safe and secure enough to be truly happy. So I said to myself that I had to move quickly and get a trap set for your guardians before you really knew what was going on. All you needed was just a little more time— another day or two and you'd have it figured out, I knew—and the best time for you to realise what was going on would be just after your guardians were so convinced that they were home free and safe that they would have absolutely no shadow of a doubt. They had to be that secure to admit their guilt to me, and the fact that I'd brought you to them while fully realising their real intent was enough to convince them that I would make an excellent accomplice. So I called Darrell and helped him set up the recording device early this morning, they called then up to betray you to them. It worked beautifully.' He dropped his head into his hands, briefly, saying softly, 'I thought I was going to die.'

'And of course they weren't to know just how I escaped the second time, and that you'd helped me. But, Mike, I still don't understand. I still don't know why you did it. How could you do that to me?'

He rubbed his face tiredly with one hand and stared over it at a group of chattering people walking by. She knew that he wasn't really seeing them. 'Maybe my thinking was wrong. I don't pretend to be right. I just did what I thought would be the best in the situation I found myself in. I wanted your guardians to believe beyond a shadow of a doubt that you'd been betrayed, and I didn't have the time or the safety to test your acting abilities. No one could have acted that bitter, stunned look in your eyes this morning. It wasn't that I didn't trust you—I knew that you'd handle yourself well in any situation. I just had to be sure of your guardians' reaction. Everything depended on that, everything. If they'd doubted for one minute the utter reality of the situation, they could have taken you away legally and gotten off scot-free.'

He'd thought of everything. He'd been far ahead of her the whole time. And it had been she who had betrayed him. 'So I was the one who really didn't trust, then,' she said sadly. Mike stared at her. She explained, 'I should have known better than to think you would have given me to my aunt and uncle, and I should have searched for a reason right away instead of believing the surface facts. Oh, Mike, I'm sorry!'

'Oh, no—don't, sweetheart, please. How could you know to trust me that way? You'd learned to trust what

told you, and I said to your face that I'd betrayed you.
And if you hadn't believed me right away, I'd have lied
and told you anything but the truth. It hurt to see you
looking so wounded! I won't forgive myself for that.
Even if everything has worked out successfully, that
was terribly wrong of me. It's I who am sorry, Dee.'

She smiled at him and put a finger to his lips. 'No
more self-accusations, please!' she murmured. 'I think
we're going to have to agree to differ on this issue,
because I think I should have had more faith in you
than I did. It was such an obvious contradiction! You
were asking me last night to have faith in yourself and
not just humanity. You didn't have to say it in words. I
caught what you were really saying to me, and I failed
you. I won't ever doubt you again.'

Her eyes fell and her face became suddenly so
unhappy and uncertain that he was moved to ask,
'What's wrong, sweetheart?'

She looked away, troubled. 'Nothing, not really.
Only—oh, Mike, I do wish I knew what was going to
happen to me now!' And in the silence that fell between
them, as she waited for the reassurance that didn't
come, she began to feel really frightened at what the
future would bring.

Because she knew then. He wouldn't want to see her
any more. This really was the beginning of the end.

CHAPTER TEN

DEE stood nervously before a mirror, straightened her dress, patted her hair, then straightened her dress again. She laughed ruefully at her reflection. Today was like every other day. Today was not so different. She felt just like she had yesterday. It was foolish, the importance that was put on a certain day as opposed to any other day of the year.

Today was her birthday. She was eighteen, a legal adult. She came into a hell of a lot of money today, though the real power of her inheritance did not come to her until she was twenty-one. Today she was either going to gain a world of happiness or lose it for ever.

It would be the biggest gamble of her life.

She checked her slim gold watch for the fiftieth time. Everyone would be here in about an hour. Then she checked her reflection again, restlessly. Her gaze sharpened on herself as she realised the incredible amount of changes that she'd been through in the last eleven months. There was an expression about her eyes, an almost indefinable sense of something there, a hint of capability perhaps, or a touch of calm efficiency. It wasn't surface appearance; she felt in control of herself, and that had been one of the hardest lessons she'd learned in the last year. She looked—strong.

Yes, she thought, I've changed. What a strange thing it is, this involuntary emotional impulse the world calls love! It comes from nowhere and it takes one by surprise, and it grabs hold of the heart so securely it's impossible to shake loose. It wouldn't matter if we married, or didn't marry, or if we would marry and eventually get a divorce—or if I would never see him

162

again. I love him. All throughout the changes and the pains and highs and lows of my life, that one fact will remain immutable. It may change through the years and metamorphosise as I change and metamorphosise, but it will never die. Though you may build a life all by yourself or perhaps with someone else, and though you may have some happiness in your life, how could you ever forget that special one you cared for, loved?

She shook her head bemusedly. It was an unanswerable question to her, just as the very emotion that she was experiencing was incomprehensible to her. She did not know where it came from or why. All that she knew or cared to know was that she loved.

She checked her watch again and sighed. Aimlessly she travelled from room to room in her huge, spacious, beautiful home as she waited. The darkness that had been her depression was gone. The house was home again. She could look and remember the happiness and the love that she had shared with her family with nostalgia and a misty smile, and yet the keen edge of grief was gone, along with the unhappiness.

So much had happened in the past month and a half! Her mind still spun with the whirlwind events that had crowded her life lately. At least Judith and Howard and their accomplices had been taken care of. Certainly she would never have to see them again, and that was a huge relief.

Mr Whittaker, her solicitor and legal guardian for the past several weeks, had been wonderfully kind. He had graciously allowed her the respect and consideration she had craved, and though he went out of his way to see her several times a week, dining over at the house more often than not and spending long hours with her on the subject of her money management, he had not insisted that she move in with him and had not questioned her authority in running the house. She was given the right to act on her own discretion and judgment, like any other adult, and she had responded accordingly, growing fond of the man.

A pang of uncertainty and apprehension quivered through her and her palms were so damp that she wiped them down her skirt, grimacing. Then, running down the stairs with her silken black skirt swirling around her slim legs, she checked in the large, elegant dining room to see if the room was ready. It was, with plates set on the antique sideboard for refreshments and on the other side of the room a table set up with various drinks, both alcoholic and non-alcoholic. Then she slipped into the kitchen to keep Mary company.

One of the things that Dee had done right away after coming home was to look up the housekeeper who had been with the Jansons ever since she could remember. She'd been in luck; Mary hadn't taken another position but instead had spent the time staying with her sister and 'taking a rest'. It had been a joyous reunion and Mary, plump and greying, had eagerly agreed to come back to her former position. It was, she had said, what she'd always wanted. And so she lived with Dee and was more of a friend and companion than paid servant. It was wonderful having her back.

Hands moving quickly over the trays of refreshments that she was finishing, Mary glanced up quickly and nodded her approval to Dee. 'You look just beautiful, sweetie, but do you really think black is quite the thing to wear to your own birthday party?'

Dee threw back her head and laughed. 'I hadn't even thought of it! I just picked the dress because I liked it best of all the clothes I bought last week. Do you think it's inappropriate?' She looked down at herself, slightly crestfallen. She didn't want to change.

'Oh, no! It's simply gorgeous on you and you know it!' Mary plunked down a tray noisily and threw some utensils into the large sink. Whenever she was particularly happy, she made quite a lot of noise, happily throwing pots and pans around and usually singing at the top of her tone-deaf voice. She'd been quite noisy, of late. 'It makes you look real elegant, and it slims your figure down nice, too. That wide belt makes your waist look so tiny, I bet I could span my hands around it! You don't eat enough, my girl. I'm planning on fixing that right away. Just wait until you see what's for supper!'

Dee cowered obligingly in the face of the huge carving knife that Mary brandished cheerfully. 'But do you think I should put up my hair?' she asked uncertainly. 'Or does it look all right down?'

'You look just fine, except you're too pale. Why don't you put some blusher on, for heaven's sake?' Mary scrutinised Dee's face with an easiness born of familiarity.

'I did,' Dee grumbled goodnaturedly, putting up an involuntary hand to one cheek. 'Should I put more on, do you think?'

'Well, it certainly couldn't hurt.' The older woman paused as she eyed the younger girl in front of her and continued musingly, 'Strange sort of birthday party you're having, not knowing many of the people coming and most of them older than you by many years. Not quite what I would call fun, but then,' sniff, 'I guess as it's not my birthday, I can't be complainin'.'

'But I've already told you, Mary,' Dee explained patiently, 'it's not really a birthday party. It's just a meeting of certain people because it's my birthday, not especially for it. You'll see.'

She received a suspicious stare. 'Why will I see?'

'Because I want you to be there. Some of what we'll be discussing involves you, so you'd better hurry—and put on a pretty dress, because you'll be joining us!' She skittered for the door before Mary could get out any of the astonished expostulations that her opening and closing mouth was forming soundlessly.

Dee ran up the stairs again, nimble in spite of the high-heeled black shoes she wore, and after peering into the mirror as if she expected a nasty surprise, she grabbed her blusher compact and touched a bit more colour along her cheekbones. It was an improvement. Her watch revealed that it was a quarter till three, and guests should be arriving soon.

Another wave of pure nervousness hit her and she clasped trembling hands in front of her tightly. Strangely enough, she wasn't nervous about the unknown people that she was about to meet. What was sending her into a near panic was the thought of what Mike's reaction to her surprise was going to be. She had no idea what he would do.

The past several weeks had been strange in more ways than one. She'd continued to see Mike frequently and he more often than not dined over at the house along with Mr Whittaker, becoming good friends with the older man. But they were both occupying a strange sort of never-never-land, not really furthering their relationship and not really breaking things off.

One night, not long after the climatic confrontation with her former guardians, Mike had stayed for supper and afterwards they had spent some time in the small, intimate family room. Dee had snuggled closer to him and, after an apparent hesitation, he had put his arm around her. But eventually he had gently repelled her tentative advances, saying only that he thought that they both needed some time to reassess their lives and goals. Now that life would be going on more or less normally, they both needed breathing space.

No matter how gentle the rejection had been, it had still been rejection, and not only a sexual one but a repulsion of the closeness they had shared. It still hurt to think of that night, and the hurt was bottled up with all her uncertainties and insecurities. He had continued to see her with every sign of affection and gladness, and

that had been nice and good, but that night still stood
between them like a huge brick wall that she slammed
into every time. Mike was wonderfully supportive,
attentive, stimulating and provoking, but she couldn't
quite act normal around him, selfconsciousness making
her feel awkward. Theirs was a bizarre combination of
affectionate, intimate friendship, and a wary keeping of
distance. It was nerve-racking, to say the least. He
seemed to be waiting for something, but what she
couldn't say.

Well, today was the last day. She wouldn't wait any
longer.

She looked out her bedroom window and could see a
car approaching. It was dark green. Mike was early. It
would be nice not to have to face all the strangers
alone. Mike had no idea of what was going to happen
any more than the others. Only she and Mr Whittaker
knew. Dee skipped down the stairs and opened the
front door before he had knocked. She smiled up into
his lean, serious face.

'You're the first,' she said, slightly breathless from
both her hurry and from excitement. 'I'm glad. Come
on in.' She stepped back so that he could enter.

He looked good, very good. He wore an expensive-
looking grey tailored suit with a crisp white shirt and a
dark grey tie. His dark hair was combed neatly back
and rested well against his nicely shaped head. It
revealed the grace of bodyline from his jaw to his
temple, down to the nape of his neck and beyond to the
powerful curve of his back. As she stared at him, taking
in the green brilliance of his gleaming eyes against his
dark face, Dee felt a quiver of pure sexual awareness
and longing pierce her and had to turn away in order to
hide her face.

Then she was walking briskly down the hall and
talking busily, moving so fast that she didn't see the
hand he had stretched out to her and the movement he

had made to speak. He watched her a moment, his eyes almost reluctantly appreciative of her slim graceful figure moving down the hall. Then as she paused and glanced curiously back, he gave a small, wry shrug and smiled as he joined her. She fell silent as he approached.

'You look beautiful,' he told her softly, touching one cheek with a finger. 'But then you look beautiful every day. Really, though, was black absolutely necessary?'

'What is this?' she cried, laughing up into his face. 'Everyone thinks my black dress has some sort of deep symbolic significance! I honestly put it on because I like how it looks.'

One brow cocked, thoughtfully, and his eyes travelled leisurely down her entire length, making her flush delicately. 'Yes, well,' he drawled, 'I do see what you mean. Is it new?'

'Mm, yes. I splurged and bought some new clothes last week. Talk about feeling guilty!' she gurgled merrily, swinging away and travelling around the room they had entered, unable to keep still. 'I've learned thrifty habits in Ohio. It was a chore and a wrench to see all my hard-earned money go on clothes when I was trying so hard to save money for college, and the feeling stuck! Oh, well, it's a nice habit to get into, I suppose!'

He had a curious look on his face, she saw, as she turned a smiling glance his way. 'Strange indeed. I'm sure the money you spent wouldn't even make a dent in the inheritance you receive today.'

Sensitive on the subject, Dee flushed again, but this time from annoyance. 'That's all you can think about, isn't it?' she demanded, upset. 'My stupid money. That's all anyone can think about, it seems! God, just when I think I've found someone who'll like me just for myself and nothing else, they catch a whiff of that filthy rich stink that somehow hovers around me like a poisonous gas, and suddenly that's all they can think about! You're like all the rest——' Unable to go on, she turned and stared stonily at the wall, her slim foot tapping out her temper on the hard wood floor.

'Will you just stop it!' In two strides Mike was right beside her, turning her forcibly around and shaking her slightly. A thrill of shock and something else rippled through her at his obvious agitation. 'I meant nothing of the sort! I merely made a comment on how ironic your reaction was when today is the day you come into a fortune! It's an obvious subject, not something I dwell on day and night!' The frustration welled up in his eyes and two grim lines cut down the sides of his mouth. His hands tightened on her and then he made an obvious effort to relax. His hands fell away. 'Don't let's quarrel on your birthday, Dee. It shouldn't be. You should be happy. Look,' and his hand went to his pocket to pull out a small wrapped package, 'I've brought you a present.' He offered it to her.

Unable to resist his gesture of peace and his coaxing smile, Dee smiled and reached out, but instead of taking the present that lay in his hand, she cupped his hand with both of her own and squeezed affectionately. 'I *told* you not to buy me anything,' she scolded, but the scolding was a gentle one accompanied by a glance she couldn't quite resist at the gaily wrapped parcel.

He laughed deeply and pressed it into her hands. 'Now, I knew that to be obviously insincere. What woman in the world doesn't like to open a present? Go on—open it. I think we have the time now.'

She looked at the package and then peeped up into his face with the beginnings of a twinkle. Then, giving up to the delight of the special unknown quality that wraps every present with the magic of delight, she laughed. 'Oh, all right! But you didn't really have to, you know. I was just happy to have you here today.' Then her fingers went nimbly to the package's edges, coaxing the paper apart with a careful anticipation that made the man beside her smile to himself. The wrapping was off and discarded without another glance, and she turned the velvet box over and over in her hands with a pleasant puzzling. Jewellery? Her fingers went to the side and pulled the box open gently, and as she saw what was inside, she gave a gasp of horror and delight. Nestled in the brown velvet inside the box was a glittering, dazzling pure green emerald pendant necklace. The stone was not so large as it was simply perfect, and it seemed to catch the ray of the sunlight that filtered into the airy room, throwing them back again with a magnificent glow. 'Oh, dear lord, Mike! This is—well, it's—it's just gorgeous, but it's too——'

A hand cupped her slight chin and gently forced her mouth to close, then tilted it up so that he could stare deeply into her bemused eyes. 'Dee,' he said kindly, 'shut up. I wanted it for you and I bought it, so wear it and like it or I'll beat you! It's your birthstone, did you know?'

Her eyes went as if drawn back to the dazzling jewel in the box. 'I guess so,' she murmured abstractedly, simply staring. 'But it's so—so——'

'Beautiful,' he supplied helpfully, taking the box from her unresisting fingers and extracting the gold chain carefully. 'Wonderful, a perfect present, you'll love it for ever, thank you very much, Mike. You're welcome, Dee. Turn around and I'll put it on you. Go on, girl, turn around!'

Dazedly she complied and soon felt the cool touch of precious metal against her skin, along with the pleasing warmth of his long fingers at the nape of her neck. The necklace settled into place, and she thought she felt something brush her exposed nape, but it was gone so quickly she couldn't be sure. Her hand went up to the hollow of her throat uncertainly, her eyes winging to him doubtfully.

'Just as beautiful as I'd thought it would be,' he murmured, smiling down at her. She thought fleetingly that no dead jewel, no matter how brilliant, could match the brilliant warmth of those bright eyes. His expression altered as he saw the troubled depths in her own eyes and he said with a quick harshness, 'Cut it out, will you, for heaven's sake? I have money too, and I'm not a damned pauper, even if I haven't as much as you! It caught my eye and I bought it, and that's all there is to it! If you don't want it, then you can take it back yourself and keep the refund,' And his eyes shuttered down as he turned away, as if bored with the whole scene.

Distressed, she moved over and laid a hand on his stiff arm. 'Mike, that wasn't what I was thinking, really! It's just such a—a special gift, a really special one, and—and I don't know how to thank you for it.' She let her hand fall hopelessly to her side. He was really offended this time. She said in a small voice, 'I really am overwhelmed.'

As she watched, his rigid stance relaxed and the tenseness of his jaw loosened. He sighed, impatiently, and shook his head, then he smiled ruefully at her. 'I guess we're both a bit touchy today. Do you really like it?'

Her instant glowing smile and sparkling eyes told him so, even before her swift, 'Oh, yes, I do! Thank you so much.' And she leaned on her toes to give him a feathery kiss on his lean cheek.

Suddenly he was rigid again, she felt, as her hand rested on his shoulder for balance, then he was taking her roughly into his arms, his mouth running along her cheek and blindly seeking her lips, and they were kissing starvingly, desperately, straining to each other. Dee touched his face with both hands, emitting a slight, inarticulate moan deep in her throat and . . .

. . . The front doorbell sounded with a melodious, infuriating chime.

She was released instantly as Mike's dark head shot up, and he put her from him almost absentmindedly as the rather blind look in his eyes gradually dispelled into the realisation of his surroundings. She saw that look fade away, and could have screamed in frustration. He had broken down right then, had been out of control, and now he was back into the awareness of whatever devil was plaguing him, keeping him away from her.

Well, she thought, drawing in a deep, steadying breath, no matter. There was still the whole rest of the day, and he was with her now. It would have to be enough.

He went obligingly to answer the door for her as she suddenly flew into a panic and sped to the kitchen to make sure everything was running smoothly for Mary, dithering and delaying until the other woman finally shooed her away, in a frenzy of impatient nervousness herself. Dee helped carry in a few trays of refreshments to sit on the sideboard as Mary took care of the rest and then she went, outwardly collected, to meet the strangers who were arriving with an onslaught of punctuality.

Mr Whittaker was already there, his white head gleaming and his distinguished face sending her a look of encouragement and a welcoming smile. He came forward to take her by the hand and begin the introductions to the well dressed men and women in the room, eleven the final total.

Their names and faces blurred together in Dee's mind, as will happen when one meets so many new people, but she recognised the names and the occupations that she and Mr Whittaker had so painstakingly sought out. She glanced nervously over her shoulder at Mike as he stood by a large, unlit fireplace. He wore an assessing, alert expression, his eyes running around the room and collecting data, but as yet coming up with no answers. He looked her way and lifted a dark eyebrow as the elderly solicitor

finished the introductions. It was a strange assortment
of people. There was a representative from the Allied
Corporation, the company that Dee held the majority
of stocks in, and there was a woman representative
from the American Cancer Society. Every person
represented either the head of a certain organisation or
company, and none of the different areas of business
and enterprise seemed to have anything in common
with the other. And then of course there was Mike and
Mr Whittaker, and Mary would be joining the group
shortly.

The group was soon chatting politely to one another
and to her, but for the life of her she couldn't remember
what was said. Mary soon joined the group and was
promptly introduced all around, and if there were a few
discreet eyebrows lifted at her presence in the group,
everyone was too polite to say anything about it.

In the painful process of mingling and being generally
polite to people she didn't personally know or give a
hoot about, Dee found herself temporarily alone and
was about to make her way to the sideboard for
something to quench her parched throat when a voice
drawled behind her, 'Here. I thought you were looking
a bit dazed and wilted. This should help.' Mike pressed
a glass of light wine into her hand and she accepted it
thankfully. He continued smoothly, 'I'm playing
bartender to the group.'

She started. 'Oh, I forgot! I meant to ask you but got
so flustered it just went right out of my head. Thank
you. And you're right—I needed this.' She glanced
around and then gulped unobtrusively at the beverage,
aware of the alert, watching man beside her.

'Hell of a birthday party you invited me to,' he said
conversationally, keeping his voice low enough so that
no one else could hear. 'That was what you had said it
was to be, a birthday party, or did I hear you wrong on
the phone?'

She started to feel uncomfortable. He was watching her so sternly and so strangely near to hostility that she was beginning to feel distinctly ill at ease. The fact that his puzzled suspicion was warranted didn't help. 'Yes, well,' she coughed, 'I thought it was about time to meet some people that—that my parents knew some years back, and——'

'Come off it, sweetheart,' he said, his anger pulsing beneath the surface politeness. 'You're cooking up something in that pretty little head of yours, and I've learned to be very wary when you do that. And for some unfathomable reason, it has something to do with me. I don't know what's going on, and I don't like that feeling. It makes me feel uncomfortable. What the hell is going on?'

Dee decided that the best strategy at the moment would be a fast, prudently surreptitious retreat, and said quickly, 'Now is this the way to mingle socially? Come on, Mike, I'm counting on you to help me make the guests feel comfortable . . .' She took a few nimble steps back as out of the corner of her eye she saw the woman from the Cancer Society come their way, an appreciative gleam in her eye as she gazed at Mike. He was neatly caught as he sent Dee a brief, furious glance before turning his attention to the woman beside him.

It was time. She couldn't take much more of this nervous excitement, and she signalled to Mr Whittaker with her eyes. He caught the look, nodded to her reassuringly, and stepped into an open space to gain everyone's attention.

'Ladies and gentlemen,' he started out formally, clearing his throat. 'We are very pleased that you were all able to make it here today, and we know you must all be feeling justifiably mystified at the reason why you were all invited. If you all would be so kind as to have a seat at the table over here . . .' An ensuing quiet scuffle arose at that as everyone slowly filed over obligingly to sit down at the huge mahogany table. Dee moved over to the end seat and sat down silently, putting her wine glass in front of her. Her head turned as she looked to see where Mike was heading, and she saw him start her way, still with that stern expression on his face. He was forestalled by something the woman said to him, and by the time he had turned around again, the president of the board of directors at Allied had seated himself at her left while a man whom she couldn't remember seated himself at her right. She noted that Mike had finally located a spot about halfway down the table, then she turned her attention to Mr Whittaker, who had taken up the position at the head of the table.

'. . . thank you very much.' He paused and cleared his throat again, then looked towards Dee. Very much aware of the close attention that she was receiving from Mike and, incidentally, everyone else in the room, she nodded slightly and the older man began. 'You have all met your hostess, Deirdre Janson, the daughter of the late millionaire Charles Janson. He was the man who started Allied Corporation and built up the business into the multi-million-dollar operation it is today. What most of you do not know is that today is Miss Janson's eighteenth birthday and the day that she legally comes into the bulk of her inheritance.'

A buzz of conversation murmured around the room and Dee responded somehow to the expressed good wishes of various people, but she wasn't really paying attention to them. Pale and tense, she kept her eyes on Mike as he shot her a narrowed, keen glance. She kept her eyes on him.

Mr Whittaker quietly continued, 'Several weeks ago, Deirdre asked me to look into the various organisations that you all represent here today and to collect information on each one's goal and financial status . . .' She could see a muscle bunch in Mike's jaw.

He was as tense, then, as she was. '. . . which I was quite willing to comply with. Then, after learning what I had to tell her about you all, she requested something of me that was so incredible, I at first did not credit her with being totally serious. After many hours of discussion, though, I realised that she was utterly sincere and adamant, so I reluctantly started the rather lengthy procedures that managing such a huge estate entails. Thus, on the date of her legal acquisition of her inheritance, she is able with little delay to dispense with her fortune as she sees fit.' He put on a pair of gold-rimmed eye-glasses, and while he rummaged around in his coat pockets, the room was so still one could have heard a pin drop. Dee was still watching Mike and saw him turn rigidly white. Mr Whittaker asked gently, 'Would you like to carry on, my dear?'

She started as if coming out of a trance and murmured, 'No, thank you.'

'Very well,' and he pulled out a sheet of white paper and studied it for a moment before continuing. 'Without further preamble, here are the final figures that Miss Janson has decided to contribute to you. To the American Cancer Society, she wishes to contribute the sum of five million dollars, to be used specifically for research purposes and the relief of the huge medical costs for cancer-stricken families. To the Blue Cross, she wishes to contribute the sum of four million dollars, to be used as the administration sees fit. To the National Aeronautic Space Administration, she wishes to contribute the sum of four million dollars, to be specifically used for space exploration and research. To the . . .' And so the list went, as Mr Whittaker's dry, unemotional voice read the distribution of the source of all Dee's former unhappiness. She didn't listen; she'd heard it all before, time and time again, as they'd thrashed out the exact sums of the money she was handing away so freely. She was experiencing at the moment a huge relief to be free of the heavy burden her inheritance had been, and a terrified reaction to Mike's silent, white, rock-carven face and leaping eyes. She didn't even hear the incredulous gasps from everyone else or the ejaculations of astonishment her bombshell had induced.

Mr Whittaker was finishing. '. . . and finally, the bulk of the rest of the inheritance, which is around six million dollars, is to go to the workers at Allied Corporation, to be specifically used for better insurance coverage and retirement benefits, and safety procedures. Miss Janson has expressed the wish to me that on her twenty-first birthday she wishes to sign over all her controlling stock to the workers of Allied Corporation on the stipulation that the controlling power of the stock shares is to be used by the board of directors only, while the profits are to be put back into the company to benefit the workers and the business. Miss Janson is keeping enough money for the complete and permanent upkeep of this house, together with a pension plan for her housekeeper, Mary Janusinski, and enough money to send her through college, but it's a mere fraction of the money she's just handed to you all on a silver platter. In essence, ladies and gentlemen, she's just given away twenty-three million dollars.' And in the amazed and delighted uproar that followed these words, no one heard him say softly as he sat heavily down, 'And a more lunatic and wonderful act I've yet to see!'

Dee was swamped with the effusive thanks and delighted exclamations. She felt bowled over with the concerted rush everyone made to shake her hand, and it was a few minutes before she could look up to see where Mike was. He wasn't in his seat, so her eyes flew around the room and she found him casually pouring a drink on the other side of the room and handing it gallantly to the woman from the Cancer Society. His face was bland and calm and so utterly normal that at

first she felt a sharp disappointment. Then he looked up
and glanced her way, and she caught the banked-down
emotion in those violently leaping expressive eyes. Still,
it was impossible to gauge the extent or exact nature of
his reaction, and she felt suddenly, totally flat.

After an eternity of chatter and the nightmare of
bearing patiently with everyone's bubbling gratitude,
she finally felt that she could take the chance to sneak
away for a breath of fresh air.

A smiling, quick glance around the room placed
everyone's position in her mind, and a minute or so of
alert scrutiny presented a moment when everyone, for
some reason or another, was looking away from the
direction of the door. Dee nimbly made her escape. Out
in the hall she sent one brief, longing glance towards the
closed front door, imagining momentarily with a sharp
pang the feeling of utter freedom and flight, and the
exhilarating excitement of the chase. She smiled,
touched the necklace that caressed the hollow of her
slim throat, and sedately walked into the small family
room, towards the back of the house. She checked her
watch and guessed five minutes.

Mike made it there in three.

Her head jerked swiftly to the door as she heard the
sound of approaching footsteps. They paused outside
the closed door and then the knob was turned and the
door opened silently. He slipped through quietly,
checking the hall before shutting the door behind him.
Then, as he turned to face her, sitting with a credible
appearance of calm in a high-backed armchair, his hand
went to the door and locked it deliberately.

That made her heart start to thump with surprise and
consternated uncertainty. With lifted golden eyebrows,
she watched him lean casually against the door, one
foot kicked over the other, hands folded across his
chest, and an implacable, unfathomable look on his
utterly serious face. His jaw was tight, she could see. A

muscle bunched spasmodically and then relaxed. They're beginning to wonder where you are,' he commented offhandedly.

Dee expelled a sudden, explosive breath and the pressure of the moment made her answer snappily, 'So what? I'm entitled to my privacy, like everyone else. They were all smothering me!' And she caught her breath at the controlled frustration in her voice.

He didn't move and his expression didn't shift or change. And with that flat, unemotional voice that gave her absolutely no hint as to what his feelings were, he asked her, 'Why did you do it?'

She just looked at him, large eyes black with dilated strain, darkly sparkling against the perfect background of her golden hair and pale skin. She swallowed, and the glittering gem at her throat winked. 'I didn't want the money.'

One brow lifted, sardonically, and he remained silent, his expression extremely sceptical, goading. She resented that look, and she retorted, 'Don't look at me that way, damn it! I've no earthly reason to lie to you or anyone else about it! It was a dead weight around my neck, always present, always constricting, always the source of my unhappiness—it's caused me nothing but grief and pain and trouble—ever since my parents died. It's been the mire that bogged me down so that I couldn't be free!'

Something quivered across his face and flickered away, so fast she couldn't define it. He seemed to hesitate and search for words, then he asked her carefully, 'Why is it always the source of your unhappiness? Why was it making you unhappy now? You'd everything ahead of you, the freedom and respect from your guardian, the immense freedom of being wealthy enough to do whatever you wanted ... what's made you unhappy now?'

As realisation hit her of what she had just given

away, she flinched physically and then instinctively retreated into a shell of uncommunicative silence simply sliding away into herself, quivering in her chair like a caught and frightened rabbit. And even while she reacted so involuntarily she berated herself for not being able to take that final, declarative step.

Across the room she heard a violent exclamation, but she didn't catch what was said—and then suddenly Mike was right on the floor in front of her chair, reaching convulsively for her trembling hands. But everything about Dee was trembling, and not just her hands: her shoulders, her mouth, her whole body quivered. Then he was looking up at her, so dear and familiar and strong, wonderfully, masculinely strong, nd she couldn't stop herself from falling forward, right into his arms. They closed around her with an eager swiftness, crushing her tight against him, and as her face instinctively burrowed into the front of his shirt, she felt his face come down with a great sigh and nestle in her hair.

'Dear, sweet, unpredictable, crazy girl,' he murmured, running both hands up and down her back. She hiccuped an incoherent response, meaning vaguely to say something intelligent but only managing an inarticulate mumble. He whispered to her, 'Shall I tell you what I think? I think you meant every word you just said to me, but there's something you haven't yet told me. I think that there's only one explanation for the reason you invited me here today to witness what just happened. I was the only one besides Mr Whittaker who wasn't a beneficiary. There was no practical reason for my presence, was there, sweetheart? Except maybe one insane, wild, improbable reason ... Dee, look at me.'

It was an impossible request. She shook her head frantically, twisting her hands into his shirt and probably ruining the material quite irreparably, but either really noticed as he put both hands gently on he sides of her head and forced her to meet his incredible, warm eyes. And of course once she looked at him she couldn't look away but instead drank in greedily that telltale emotion that spilled from his glowing gaze.

'That money has made you impossibly touchy for some time now,' he went on slowly, still with that look of incredulity lingering. 'And we both know that it's made me more than edgy. I wanted to give you time, time to readjust to a normal life without always having to look over your shoulder and be afraid. I wanted to a give you the chance for freedom if you wanted it, and chance to realise the enormous potential that your inheritance would bring you. I didn't want to restrict you in any way. And oh, God, I wanted to have you so!' He closed his eyes and brought down his mouth to drink caressingly from her willing lips. Then he said with a thread of unsteady laughter, 'Deirdre, my mad darling girl, I love you quite passionately and always will, and I probably would have gotten around to telling you fairly soon, but did you have to chuck the whole bloody bundle right out the window to prod me to it?'

Dee exploded into a breathless laugh and pressed her lips to him again and again, and of course Mike was responding quite eagerly, and the closeness and the wonderful warmth of him was everything she'd known it would be. Then, leaning back against the curve of his arm and laughing brilliantly up into his face, emotion making her eyes almost impossibly black and blue and white against a pink flush of happiness, she said, gurgling merrily, 'You've carried your deduction admirably far, but you haven't reached the whole of it quite yet.' He smiled involuntarily at her deliberate use of words which brought to mind their last confrontation, now several weeks ago. 'At first, several weeks ago, I was desperate enough to think of the Big Gesture, but thought about it more and more and I realised that really didn't want the money. It became a matter of— well, I just wanted to be rid of the whole mess. The rea gamble was how you'd react to such an action, no' necessarily the actual donations. I love you. I don' want anything to come between us, ever. But I stil don't think you realise that I *like* to balance my own chequebook every week, and I *like* to earn a pay-cheque by my own sweating effort. My father's success was wonderful, but it's not my success, and I want to taste success the striving, climbing, hard way, the real way. I'm not the same person who so blithely skipped out of town all those months ago. I'm different, and I'm older, and I've freely chosen a different way of life, without pressure from you or anyone else.'

His finger ran over her face lightly, lovingly, and he breathed, incredibly to her mind, disgustedly, 'At every turn, every single damned time, I've managed to underestimate you. You wonderful, lovable lunatic! Dare I assume that you're going to marry me, love, or did you have something else in mind?'

She sent him a look. 'What do you think?' Her eyes twinkled at him as he laughed, head thrown back, hair falling off his brow.

He moved off the floor, bent and slid his arms around her, and picked her up as lightly as if she had been a child. Then he moved over to the couch and sat down, firmly holding her against his chest as if he would never let her go. Dee put her head down on his shoulder, and his arms tightened convulsively. 'I never want to let you go, never want to see you walk out of my life,' he muttered, deep in his throat, staring straight ahead. She held very still, instinctively recognising in that low tone something important. 'Dee,' he whispered, and the whispering was both a plea and a command, 'I need you. I need your

armth and your gaiety, and your zest for adventure
nd life. I'm too old for you.'

At that she moved in an instinctive protest, her
ntention to deny it, contradict what he'd say in that
ow, serious voice. He looked down at her and held her
uiet with his eyes.

'But I'm a selfish man, and always have been,' he
ontinued, self-mockery evident in his manner. 'And
'm not about to let you go.' His green eyes were gently
miling at her, and her throat felt constricted suddenly
vith emotion.

'Don't you know even now?' she whispered, her eyes
a brilliant, sparkling wet blue as she stared up at him.
Don't you know that I need you every bit as much,
eed your love? That without it, my life is as barren as a
esert?'

But Mike was shaking his head at that and smiling
strangely. 'Oh, no. No, you're one of those special
people who never have a barren life, because of the
quality in them that makes them reach out and grasp
what there is in life with both eager hands.'

'And you're not?' Dee queried laughingly. 'I can't
and won't believe that! Not in your line of work, not in
your profession! You've reached out every bit as eagerly
for that special life—and that's one of the reasons why I
love you so.'

'Yes,' he mused, leaning his head back on the couch,
'I've led a pretty full life. I've had some experiences as a
private investigator, let me tell you! It was a good time.'

She stared at him, alarmed. 'You're—you're talking
as if it's over,' she managed to get out, hesitantly. His
eyes slanted down to her roguishly.

'It is,' he said simply, and waited for her explosion.
Dee surprised him yet again by simply staring, finally
managing to get out something that sounded quite
strangled.

'I—don't understand,' she whispered.

His eyes looked amused, and it was a gentl amusement that caressed her. 'Deirdre my sweet,' h murmured in a loving mockery, 'my line of work ha been rough, with its fair share of risks. I've don some harrowing things in the last few years, not t mention running into a burning building, nearl getting shot—twice, I believe—and fighting for m life and yours in near-pitch darkness with tw opponents. Before I had only myself to think of, and now I have you. There's one thing I never want fo you to experience. I never want for you to get phone call, or a late night visit from kindhearted reluctant policemen, and that would be a possibility if I didn't quit now. I love you—I want to spend m life with you. Listen to what I'm saying, Dee. They're simple words, but they have an overwhelming precedence in my mind.'

He shook her up so. Her eyes really were blurred, as she looked away, feeling somehow terribly sad and incredibly touched.

'I have money invested,' he said, continuing cheerfully after one intense, quick scrutiny of her face and expression. 'It's a fair amount—quite enough to draw an annual income from, in fact. After you finish school and have a better idea of what direction your career life is going to be heading in, I think we should consider traveling around a bit. I've always wanted to have adventures overseas. Then perhaps I can think about setting up a detective agency, and put my administrative college courses to use.'

Dee began to brighten. 'That's an idea. I could be your secretary.'

'Can you type?'

'N—no.'

'We'll work on it,' he told her kindly, and laughed at her expression. He pressed his lips to her forehead before continuing. 'You say you want to taste success on your own steam. I think you've demonstrated adequately this afternoon that money can't be your goal. Just suppose you were to make a fortune on your own—what in the world would you do with it?'

She ruefully grimaced and laughed. 'I just got rid of one headache and here you are trying to give me another one! I really doubt that I would do that—I'm the world's worst businessperson. In fact, I don't really know what kind of success or lifestyle that I want to work for, yet! I think I'll just be happy to be happy, no matter what I do. And I know,' and she snuggled down closer to him, 'that I'm going to be happy. But if by some bizarre chance I made a fortune in money, why——' her eyes twinkled coyly up at his and slipped away, '—I guess I'd give it all away and do it again.'

The swooping, laughing, unrestrained hug that she got from him at that was so full of a wealth of joyous warmth and love that she wordlessly knew she'd already found her fortune, and it was more than enough for her. Mike grabbed her head, pulled her around, and he started to kiss her strongly, hungrily, and she suddenly felt the piercing ache that had been inspired by weeks without him. They were both so totally swept away with their own wants and needs that she felt more than a little out of control, and shaken.

He broke off kissing her, leaned his head into the hollow of her slender neck and shoulder, one hand jerkily massaging her shoulder. And then she felt him smile, felt his chest heave slightly, and she smiled to herself, murmuring, 'What? What is it? Tell me.'

Mike turned his head and whispered into her ear, 'I must confess to some ambitions, even though you are so singularly free from them.'

'Mm. What are they?' she asked, not really paying attention since his hands were distracting her so deliciously. He brought his lips even closer and delicately nipped her ear before whispering something into her ear that made her eyes start open wide, her heart thud hard, and she laughed breathlessly. 'You're kidding! Tonight? Oh, my, you are an ambitious fellow, aren't you?'

Take these
4 best-selling novels
FREE

Yes! Four sophisticated, contemporary love stories by four world-famous authors of romance FREE, as your introduction to the Harlequin Presents subscription plan. Thrill to **Anne Mather**'s passionate story BORN OUT OF LOVE, set in the Caribbean.... Travel to darkest Africa in **Violet Winspear**'s TIME OF THE TEMPTRESS....Let **Charlotte Lamb** take you to the fascinating world of London's Fleet Street in MAN'S WORLD .... Discover beautiful Greece in **Sally Wentworth**'s moving romance SAY HELLO TO YESTERDAY.

Harlequin Presents...

The very finest in romance fiction

Join the millions of avid Harlequin readers all over the world who delight in the magic of a really exciting novel. EIGHT great NEW titles published EACH MONTH! Each month you will get to know exciting, interesting, true-to-life people .... You'll be swept to distant lands you've dreamed of visiting .... Intrigue, adventure, romance, and the destiny of many lives will thrill you through each Harlequin Presents novel.

Get all the latest books before they're sold out!
As a Harlequin subscriber you actually receive your personal copies of the latest Presents novels immediately after they come off the press, so you're sure of getting all 8 each month.

Cancel your subscription whenever you wish!
You don't have to buy any minimum number of books. Whenever you decide to stop your subscription just let us know and we'll cancel all further shipments.

Your FREE gift includes

- MAN OF POWER by **Mary Wibberley**
- THE WINDS OF WINTER by **Sandra Field**
- THE LEO MAN by **Rebecca Stratton**
- LOVE BEYOND REASON by **Karen van der Zee**

Harlequin Photo Calendar

Turn Your Favorite Photo into a Calendar.

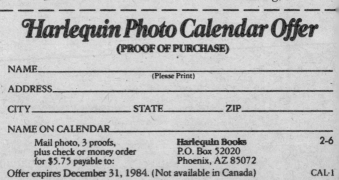

Uniquely yours, this 10 x 17½" calendar features your favorite photograph, with any name you wish in attractive lettering at the bottom. A delightfully personal and practical idea!

Send us your favorite color print, black-and-white print, negative, or slide, any size (we'll return it), along with **3** proofs of purchase (coupon below) from a June or July release of Harlequin Romance, Harlequin Presents, Harlequin Superromance, Harlequin American Romance or Harlequin Temptation, plus $5.75 (includes shipping and handling).